the Second Mango

by Shira Glassman

The Second Mango by Shira Glassman, ed. by Jessica St. Ama

Queen Shulamit never expected to inherit the throne of the tropical land of Perach so young. At twenty, grief-stricken and fatherless, she's also coping with being the only lesbian she knows after her sweetheart ran off for an unknown reason. Not to mention, she's the victim of severe digestive problems that everybody thinks she's faking. When she meets Rivka, an athletic and assertive warrior from the north who wears a mask and pretends to be a man, she finds the source of strength she needs so desperately.

Unfortunately for her, Rivka is straight, but that's okay — Shulamit needs a surrogate big sister just as much as she needs a girlfriend. Especially if the warrior's willing to take her around the kingdom on the back of her dragon in search of other women who might be open to same-sex romance. The real world outside the palace is full of adventure, however, and the search for a royal girlfriend quickly turns into a rescue mission when they discover a temple full of women turned to stone by an evil sorcerer.

Cover art by Erika Hammerschmidt and Jane Dominguez

Psalms 23:1-2, as translated by Dr. Alana M. Vincent, Lecturer in Jewish Studies, Department of Theology & Religious Studies, University of Chester, UK
Esther 7:3 as translated by Dr. Alana M. Vincent, Lecturer in Jewish Studies, Department of Theology & Religious Studies, University of Chester, UK

Siegfried, by Richard Wagner, 1876, Act II as translated by Shira Glassman: *Wer bist du, kühner Knabe, der das Herz mir traf?* in one of the hetero love scenes. Don't Google this unless you want a surprise spoiled.

All quoted literature sourced from the public domain.

*Dedicated to my good friend Anastasia "Ducky" Newcamp,
and in memory of my father.*

❀ • ❀ • ❀

Chapter 1: The Northerner

Once upon a time, in a lush tropical land of agricultural riches and shining white buildings, there was a young queen who spent the night tied up in a tent, panicking.

Apparently, a visit to a bawdy house got you kidnapped.

That wasn't entirely accurate. Queen Shulamit was sure that plenty of men went in and out of such places every night without so much as losing a hair on their heads. But a skinny woman of barely twenty — even one who had been queen of Perach for two whole months — well, that was a different story. Especially if that young queen had ditched her bodyguards and snuck out by herself.

It didn't feel real. Shulamit had the same numb feeling she had gotten two months earlier, when they'd first told her that her father was going to die. *But can't I go back to yesterday?* She visualized herself turning a page backward in a book, undoing her part in the events of the previous evening.

She wondered if her bodyguards were close to finding her. She knew they were looking — the queen's safety was their entire career. They were probably very frustrated with her right now, and she couldn't blame them. That is, if they even knew where she was. The only sign they had of where she'd gone was her frantic scream — "I'm the queen! Tell the palace! *Get help!*" — to two of the so-called "willing women" as she was carried away wrapped in a bolt of cloth.

Eventually, she knew from eavesdropping, someone from the court would have to ransom her if she wasn't rescued. How long would that take? She'd been tied up in the tent like this for hours, long enough that fear and shame had been joined by boredom and hunger. Her stomach gnawed at itself, but she was worried that

1

even if her kidnappers gave her something to eat, she'd throw up or — or worse.

One comfort was that she was still wearing all of her clothes, and, blissfully, the men guarding her were ignoring her at the moment. She felt thankful for her average looks. If the men had gone anywhere near her *like that* —

She was roused from her self-absorbed stupor by noises outside the brigands' tent. Maybe they were fighting over whether or not to rape her after all, instead of just worrying about money. *Please, Aba, no, no. Please send someone to rescue me.* Or maybe there was a mutiny in the ranks! That sounded much better.

Or maybe the commotion was caused by the big blond warrior wearing a cloth mask over the bottom half of his face who now burst into the tent, scattering sleepy guards with a fist and a gigantic sword.

"I hope you're on my side," Shulamit found herself saying, frightened anew by his foreignness. Like all of her people, her skin was medium brown, but this man's was much lighter, and his body was taller and bulkier than even most of her guards. Where had he come from?

"*Malka*? Queen?"

"No, I'm the head kidnapper," Shulamit snapped. "How do you like my Queen Shulamit costume? I'm practicing for my singing debut." Was this stranger out for his own ends, stealing from thieves and kidnapping from kidnappers? That would make it even harder for her bodyguards to track her down.

"Very funny. No, I'm not one of the bad guys. I'm your hired help." The warrior was already untying her bonds, tugging at ropes and slicing them with a dagger in places where the brigands had gotten virtuosic with their knots. "Are you unharmed?"

2

"For the most part." Shulamit studied the warrior. "Who are you?" His brown leather tunic was sleeveless, leaving plenty of room for the powerful muscles of his upper arms. Hair exploded in a messy tangle of several yellows from the base of his helmet down past his shoulders. His thick, sleek eyebrows were darker than his hair, and his speech was accented — although the northern folk used the same alphabet, their language was different.

"I'm Riv." There was a respectful pause, and a bow from the neck. "Mercenary and bounty hunter. I travel, I fight — I do what needs doing. Your bodyguards are out looking for you, but since they wanted you back before anyone else knew you'd been taken, they also hired *me*. Lucky for them!"

"Lucky for me," added Shulamit. "You're... from the north?"

"You can tell?" Riv smirked. "I think I got all the knots. Let's go!"

Shulamit barely had time to brace herself nervously for such intimate contact with the body of a strange man before Riv scooped her up into his mighty arms and flung her over his shoulder. He carried her out of the tent, pausing here and there to launch powerful kicks at the surprised brigands, but mostly running all the way. The next thing Shulamit knew, she had been plunked down roughly onto the back of an enormous horse, bigger than any she'd ever seen, and Riv had leapt up behind her. The horse immediately broke into a run.

But the men who had kidnapped her had horses too. "They're gaining on us," Shulamit pointed out.

"No, they're not."

The horse reared on its back legs, sending Shulamit backward into Riv's torso. Then they were suddenly rising away from the ground, and the horse had turned green. A robust and powerful wave of muscle on each side pushed them farther into the air.

3

Shulamit hadn't expected the horse to fly, and she certainly hadn't expected green wings either —

"But this was a *horse!*"

"And now she's a dragon. And you're a freed prisoner. Congratulations." Riv looked self-satisfied and patted the dragon's side. As a dragon, the beast was even larger; certainly big enough to carry the two of them, and maybe even a third person. Her scales were a deep, dark green, and textured, like a jeweled avocado rind, and they covered most of her, except the short, stubby horns on her head, which were a dull gold, like dirty jewelry. Two enormous wings, angular and with pointed tips like a bat's, stuck out from her sides and propelled them through the air. Beyond Riv at the back of the dragon, the queen caught glimpses of a powerfully muscled tail.

Shulamit was entranced — she'd never seen a dragon this close before. In fact, she hadn't seen a dragon since her father's fiftieth birthday celebration several years ago, when lots of exotic and exciting things were brought to the palace for the general amusement of its residents. She had liked it then and had wanted a closer look, but her father was concerned for her safety and wouldn't permit her to observe it from anywhere except the dais from which they watched the aerial performance. How ironic, considering the great man had never thought elephants unsafe as long as you weren't underfoot. Shulamit hadn't had any reason to disagree until the day her father fell off the one he was riding during his return from a diplomatic visit. She had a horror of elephants now. But she still loved dragons, and this one was first-rate.

She peered around the countryside, where the first rays of sun glittered over the palm trees. "Wow, they really took me a long way outside the city."

"Did your captors give you any food?" Riv asked.

"I haven't eaten all night."

"There's a pita in my bag."

"Thanks, but I can't," said the queen sadly.

"Can't?"

Shulamit didn't answer. If her own servants didn't believe her about her food problems, what hope had she with a stranger? After her ordeal, she certainly didn't have the energy to argue.

The beast swerved upward slightly, shifting against the wind, and Shulamit once again slid backward against Riv's chest. What she thought she felt the first time she'd crashed into Riv upon liftoff was definitely there, confirming her suspicions. "Your dragon's not the only one of you who's hiding things."

There was only silence behind her as Riv waited for her to continue — apparently, too seasoned to finish Shulamit's thoughts for her, in case the little queen was bluffing.

"You're a woman."

"What if I am?"

"You're a woman dressed as a man." Shulamit's mind was racing, and she whirled her head around to face her rescuer. "Does that mean you seek women for love... like I do?" The words tumbled out impulsively, the child of a night without affection and a morning without breakfast. From beneath her thick, dark brows she gazed into Riv's undeniably foreign gray-blue eyes and tried to look as alluring as an underslept hungry person could possibly manage.

Riv laughed, her face relaxing, probably relieved that she wasn't having her reputation or skill challenged. "No, it does not," said Riv. "Except as friends, of course, and I think maybe we're already friends."

"Oh." Shulamit was still too tired and her stomach too empty — or possibly, she was too much a monarch — to be anything but blunt. "I mean, yes — yes, we can be friends."

"Careful — your sadness is bringing down the dragon," said Riv. It took Shulamit a moment to realize Riv was only teasing. "By the way, I'm really Rivka. But don't let anyone else hear that, Your Majesty."

"You're a very good fighter," said Shulamit, still feeling rather awkward as she turned back around to face forward, her neck hurting from craning around for so long. She was riding pressed very close to the chest of this person and confused over whether or not it was okay to enjoy herself, now that she knew definitely that Rivka was not interested.

"Thank you! I know, as a paid mercenary, it's probably none of my business, but as a new friend... that wonderful retinue of bodyguards you keep — how did you manage to get stolen from under their noses?"

Shulamit sighed. "I wasn't under their noses. I snuck out." If only her bodyguards would stop acting like baby-sitters and had agreed to go with her. How aggravating it was that they hadn't allowed her to go — especially since it would have meant an excuse to venture inside themselves under the pretext of chaste employment. Any man would welcome that! Well, most men, anyway.

Shulamit reasoned that if there were women like her who sought other women — and she'd had a sweetheart once, so she knew she wasn't the only one, even if Rivka wasn't one of them — there must be men who sought other men. Once she was out of her current predicament, she wondered if she shouldn't fire all her bodyguards and find some of that sort. Surely, *they* would understand and not go around constantly trying to protect her from herself.

Rivka's jaw dropped. "All this trouble—"

"I know, I know! And I'm sorry." Shulamit sighed, apologizing silently once again to her dead father. This was not how she was supposed to be ruling from his throne. "I just — I wanted—" She paused for a moment, knowing she probably shouldn't be talking about her indiscretions. On the other hand, Rivka was the first real ally she'd had since Aviva's disappearance, and besides, she held Rivka's secret herself, so it was likely Rivka wouldn't talk. "I went to a bawdy house. I don't have a sweetheart—"

"You know what you do have? You have a hole in the head," said Rivka, trying to sound cross but with a strong feeling of indulgent pity coming through anyway. "Pardon my directness, Your Majesty, but why not just ask for a woman to be brought in — if a young queen really has to pay for love to begin with?"

"My bodyguards are still loyal to my father, may he rest, and not to me. They wouldn't bring a woman in, or escort me there themselves, either. I loved my father, but I don't agree with all of his rules."

Rivka took so long to respond that for a moment, Shulamit was nervous that she'd said something wrong. Then, finally, Rivka snorted, almost to herself, "To get between a young lady and her first kiss."

"I have had that," Shulamit pointed out. "That, and more." She tensed up, half in defiance, half in fear, waiting for Rivka to disapprove.

"I don't condemn you, Your Majesty," said Rivka. "I've never even kissed a man, but I've lived it all in my heart."

"If you've never — I — how do you know you like men at all?" Shulamit asked, hope creeping back into her face.

"He's dead."

"Oh. I'm sorry." Shulamit looked down. "Mine ran away. I mean — the woman I loved."

7

Rivka patted her gently on the head. "Begging your pardon for my familiarity, of course, Your Majesty."

"I'd really like to find a new love," said Shulamit. "But I don't know how to find someone else who's different like I am. That first time was a happy accident. So I brought gold to a bawdy house to buy a woman's favors. The only favor I got was about five seconds of looking at her bare bosom. Then I was carried off."

Rivka exhaled loudly through her nose.

"Do you think there are many women like me?"

"I have no idea," said Rivka. "This is the first time I ever really sat down and talked with someone like you."

Shulamit was silent for a long while, knitting up an idea in her mind. Several moments were punctuated only with the sound of the dragon's flapping wings.

Then, the queen broke the silence. "Do you want to be a warrior forever?"

Rivka answered right away. "Combat is my passion. Doing good is my mission. And feeding my face and keeping the horse in grain, of course."

Shulamit's voice changed. Suddenly, she was *Malka Shulamit bat Noach*, Queen of Perach. "In that case, I have a mission for you — if you accept. I'll find a way to make you Captain of my Guard if you'll find me a woman to cherish, and who'd cherish me in return."

Chapter 2: The Agreement

The sun had crept high and was melting its way back down the brilliant blue sky when Rivka crossed the palace green to the queen's private garden. She was still in her male disguise, despite the way the cloth made her sweat in these tropical climates far from home.

The queen was seated on velvet cushions beside the spiky-leaved pandanus trees that hung over the river. Several of her ladies-in-waiting lounged around her, but not too close, gossiping quietly. Shulamit herself was not speaking to anyone, but instead stared intently at a book in her lap as she picked at a bowl of fruit resting beside her in the grass.

The ladies-in-waiting all stared at Rivka and whispered to each other as she stalked up between them. "Your Majesty," said Rivka, bowing deeply. "One of your guards said you sent for me."

"Friends," Shulamit announced in her royal voice. "This is the man who rescued me last night. I'm grateful for his skill."

Rivka knew that despite Shulamit's obvious lack of discretion with these ladies about her own activities, the queen had kept *her* secret. "I'm glad to see you looking well, Your Majesty."

"Have my bodyguards rewarded you — generously?"

"They've been more than generous," said Rivka, whose heart was as light as her purse was now full.

"Good," said Shulamit. "Come closer. We have plans to make."

Rivka approached her. "What are you reading?"

She was expecting to hear the name of some traditional love story, or perhaps one of the more exciting, newer tales, and was taken aback when the queen answered, *"Canon of Counterfeits."*

"What?"

"It's about how to tell the difference between counterfeits and real art — gold or something adulterated with another metal — or if someone's forged an artifact of antiquity. Oh, you can sit down."

Rivka plopped down onto the grass. She had no cushion and didn't need one.

Shulamit's voice dropped so that only Rivka could hear her. "Have you thought about my proposal?"

"I have, Majesty. It would be an honor and a thrill to win that position. I'll give your quest my all, if you hold to your promise."

"I will, absolutely. I swear it. Besides, I like you." An eager expression, half-sheepish, half-seductive, slipped across her face for a moment.

"As I told you, little Queenling, *Malkeleh*, nothing happens to me when we're close. I don't feel that way about women, and I'm not the one you seek."

"*We* seek," Shulamit corrected. She held out her hand, and Rivka, still acting the male, kissed it ceremoniously and without emotion. "You win. I'll be good."

"Are none of your ladies-in-waiting interested in other women?" Rivka asked, wondering if they'd had to fight off the queen's advances too.

"Oh, *no*," said Shulamit, shaking her head slowly. "I don't even think they all understand it, entirely. I know a couple of them think that if they could just find me a prince beautiful enough, I'd stop being so strange."

"Yes, a prince with breasts," said Rivka in a low, throaty chuckle.

10

"If I think about having to touch a man that way, I feel like I'm trying to run away with my legs stuck on backwards. When I think about women it feels so natural and right and correct. I can't explain it, other than to tell you this must be how men feel. But I know I'm not a man. Despite having the smallest breasts in court, I still feel very womanly." Shulamit looked down at her spindly body, then back up at Rivka with a more businesslike expression. "Do you have any ideas about where we can find me a partner?"

"Well," Rivka began, "I gossiped with some of your bodyguards as they were waiting for you to wake up, and apparently one of them saw a show in a bawdy house where the women—"

"But that was for money," Shulamit interrupted. "That doesn't mean they like it when they're not being paid."

"And of course there are women who dress as men because they prefer to live as men, and not because it eases their career as a traveling warrior," Rivka continued glibly.

"They sound delightful! But how would I know if someone was hiding a secret like that?" Shulamit's brow furrowed. "The only reason I — it's not like I can bump into everyone's chest by mistake." She grimaced at her near slip.

"Maybe if you issued a proclamation for all the women in the land who could love the queen to come visit the palace—"

"No, no," said Shulamit, shaking her head in a tiny, frantic motion. "Think of all the ways that could go wrong. They could be men wearing dresses just to sneak into the competition; they could be women pretending to be like me but only to get at the power of the throne and not really *love* me. And my bodyguards!" She looked sick. "They'd be scandalized and nagging me constantly."

"You could order them not to," Rivka pointed out, noting not for the first time since their meeting that the queen was still so very

11

young, and acted even younger. Perhaps this is what came of a pampered and sheltered upbringing.

"Yeah, because *that's* been working out so far."

"You have to believe in your own authority if you want anyone else to," Rivka commented.

"I have another idea," said the queen, rather conspicuously changing the subject. "What if a woman didn't want to marry a man — ever — but didn't have as much freedom as I do?" Seeing a blank look in Rivka's eyes, she continued. "She could join one of the holy houses. Sure, there's the vow of poverty, a life of service... but if it were my only choice, it might almost be worth it."

"What are you talking about?"

"The celibate sisters in the temples."

"Our temples don't have celibate attendants up north, just rabbis," Rivka explained in a tense voice. Both countries celebrated the same holidays and worshipped the same One God, but naturally, the customs deviated. "Celibacy isn't part of our worship. That's for wizards..." She relaxed the fists she had unconsciously clenched.

"We have rabbis too," Shulamit explained, "but since the reign of my father's grandfather there are also temples where women can go and live by themselves."

"Huh."

"They dress very plainly — usually just a simple old robe dyed yellow with turmeric."

"Oh, yes, yes," said Rivka. "I think maybe I saw some of them without knowing what the clothing meant."

12

"Anyway, I'm sure among all the holy houses in Perach there's got to be at least one woman who's only in there so she won't have to lie down with a man against her nature."

"Didn't you say something about a celibacy vow?" Rivka slipped one hand beneath her cloth mask to wipe off a layer of sweat that had suddenly become intolerable.

"Maybe she only took the vow because she thought she didn't have any other choice," Shulamit pointed out enthusiastically. "There are at least three holy houses a few days' ride of Home City. Will you take me there, Riv? It's the best idea I've got."

Rivka thought it a fairly simplistic idea, and was concerned that Shulamit might discover nothing more than a number of women who didn't wish to be disturbed. But she could see the restless loneliness in the little queen, and it called on deeply buried needs to be asked to protect her. And neither did she have a better idea. How *should* a young woman with such... different... tastes find another like her? Rivka certainly had no idea. "You're coming with me?"

"I have to love her, don't I? Anyhow, I can't leave a decision as important as this to someone who loves only men."

"You make a good argument."

"I'll announce that I need some time in a holy house to meditate. The individual ministers of each bureau can oversee the kingdom while I'm gone — and then you and I can go searching for likely candidates for a woman to rescue!"

"If she wants rescuing," added Rivka.

"My bodyguards will probably jump for joy that I'm being so spiritual, especially after last night," said Shulamit. "They'll love the idea of you as my protection, since you've already proven that you're more than competent in keeping me out of trouble."

"I hope I can keep it up!"

13

"And your dragon as well," Shulamit added. "Can we ride her the whole way, or will she wear out?"

"She can't remain a dragon for the entire journey, but she'll be able to carry us as a mare as long as she's well treated. You're small."

Shulamit grinned weakly, more of a grimace than a smile. "I know. Sometimes when I look down at my wrists I'm shocked at how thin they are. Like I could snap in half like a stick."

"I won't let anyone snap you in half."

"Hurray, I've got hired muscle!" Now the grin was self-conscious, but happier.

The sky was darkening, and the ladies-in-waiting were picking up their cushions and brushing off the dust from the ground. "Come, Majesty," one of them called. "Come inside before the rain."

Rivka watched them flutter back toward the palace, each carrying a cushion except for the queen, who had given hers to one of the other women. She grinned and shook her head.

"Queenling," Rivka said in her own language to the droplets of rain that were beginning to fall, "There aren't any velvet cushions out there."

Chapter 3: Dawn and the Beginning of a Journey

The two women set out the following morning at dawn's first light so they could achieve a considerable distance before they were overtaken by the heat of the afternoon. Shulamit had been unable to sleep all night, her head filled with anticipation and dreams about both the journey and the woman she hoped she would meet upon it. It was therefore natural that within a few minutes of Dragon the Horse breaking into her gentle lope, the queen nodded off completely.

Rivka easily shielded her with the bulk of her body. The people of Perach were smaller in every dimension than those of the far cold north, and to the mercenary, Shulamit's body almost felt like a child's. She rode into the damp dawn air, holding back from her usual one-sided conversation with Dragon so she wouldn't disturb her sleeping passenger, and instead kept her own counsel.

❀ • ❀ • ❀

Shulamit woke when Rivka let Dragon rest in the afternoon, during the worst heat of the day. They'd stopped beside a stream flanked by coconut palms and pandanus trees. Under the uneven shade of their sword-shaped leaves, she dipped her hands in the water and wiped the dust from her eyes. "How far have we gone?"

"We're halfway to Ir Ilan," said Rivka. "We'll stay the night there, and by the next night, if we push ourselves, we should come to the first of the temples. I know it's at least a full day's ride from any settlements."

"You know your way around Perach," Shulamit remarked. She peered into the stream curiously to check if the twisted knots of

15

braided hair at the base of her neck had survived her horseback nap intact.

"I've been among your people long enough. Two years it's been since I left..." Rivka's voice sounded as though she had been about to say more to complete the thought, like "my people" or "home," or even just "the north," but then she just stopped. Behind her, the horse grazed peacefully on the bank of the stream.

There was so much Shulamit wanted to ask her that it was hard to choose where to begin. "Did you always know you wanted to be a warrior?"

Rivka smiled broadly. "As far back as I can remember. I used to pick up sticks in the courtyard of my uncle's castle and embarrass him by trying to swordfight with his guards." A sparkle like broken glass shone from her eyes, proudly defiant.

"Castle? Are you... are you of noble birth?"

"I don't know how to answer that," said Rivka. "My mother is the younger sister of the baron of our valley. My father, he was a farmhand who worked at the castle growing vegetables. She was a lot younger than you are now when they ran him out of town. You've been around palaces and the politics of reputation and decorum all your life — you can probably imagine how ashamed my uncle was that I dared to exist at all." She looked away at the horse, then back at the queen.

"It sounds so painful — but yet you're so calm when you talk about it."

"It was years ago," said Rivka, "and I have my own life and my own accomplishments to be proud of now. Believe me, I have my grievances with my uncle, and our relationship's basically beyond repair, but I found a way to forgive him on Yom Kippur. If I let my losses conquer me, I can't fight, nor smile, nor live."

"Your mother must have been a little bit like me," said Shulamit. "I had a sweetheart once, from the palace staff too. She was our palace's second cook. I love her — loved her so much sometimes I felt like I could burst open just from looking at her." Thoughts of a bosomy beauty with a goofy smile, her hair piled up on her head with a couple of sticks through it and some of it coming down around her ears unevenly, brought a tugging hunger to the queen's heart. "She was the first person to cook me food that didn't make me sick. We figured it out together, and became friends... and then... but then she acted distant and cranky, and I didn't know why, and then one day she was gone. There was a note saying that she was leaving and that I shouldn't ever try to find her or contact her. I went looking for her at her parents' house anyway, but her father said she had decided to go work as a cook somewhere else — somewhere far away. I figured if I kept looking for her after that I'd be crossing a line."

"I'm sorry that was her choice," said Rivka, "but I'm sure we'll find someone out there for you. What was that bit about food making you sick?"

Shulamit looked at her a little timidly, used to the reactions of everyone else in her life. *Oh, Princess Shulamit, her father's precious little darling, can't bear the thought of food unless it's made of solid gold and served by holy women. She pretends to be ill to look delicate.* "It started a couple of years ago. Nobody could explain it, and eventually they just decided I was shamming. Aviva — the cook I was telling you about — she fed me very pure foods one at a time until we figured out the foods my body rejects."

"Rejects?"

"Do you really want details?" Shulamit grinned hideously, frightened inside. There was a part of her that had always wondered if Aviva had left because she was unable to contain her disgust anymore. Chicken was worse than wheat — all bread did was knock her out with stomach cramps and indigestion, but

17

chicken and other fowl — she cringed with self-loathing, thinking of the mess.

"How about no. So what can't you eat?"

"The short version — fowl and wheat."

"No *wheat*?" Rivka's eyes widened. "No — no pita, no... and wait, no chicken soup when you're sick?!"

Shulamit nodded. "Tell me about it. So I make do. I've learned little tricks — when I eat flesh, or cooked vegetables, for that matter, I have to make sure the cooking surface hasn't seen a fowl, or has been cleaned recently."

"Sounds complicated. How can you tell what's making you sick? Are you sure you're not being poisoned? The king of Imbrio—"

Shulamit shook her head. "No, that was the first thing they tested, when my father was still alive. I was the only person who got sick — nothing was wrong with the food. Then he hired a magician, because he thought it might be a curse. But the magician said I wasn't under any spells, and after that, nobody believed me anymore. The whole court decided it was all in my mind and gave up on solving it. The head cook even tried to trick me into eating the things that were making me sick — she was convinced that if I didn't know it was there, the symptoms would go away."

"I'm guessing it didn't work."

"Then finally, after days of pain and not being able to keep anything down, Aviva came to me with nothing but a glass of water. She said that's where we were going to start, and we'd try adding back foods one at a time, prepared simply, until something made me sick. Then we'd know for sure what it was."

What Aviva had actually said was, *We'll add one new food or ingredient each day until we've found all the eggs the chickens have hidden in the grass.* Her colorful speech complemented the

18

rainbow of food stains across her clothing, mostly the brilliant orange-gold of turmeric.

"So what are you going to do about food when we get to Ir Ilan?" Rivka's brow furrowed. "I doubt the local inns want you nosing around in the kitchen inspecting the pans, and you won't be able to control stray wheat flour."

"I know. I've been dreading their reaction all morning. People never believe me, and then they lie and say they've done what I asked them to do when they haven't, and I have no way to tell until—" She waved her hand around helplessly.

"What about the public market? With the open stalls, you can watch the food cook and then just pick the ones who are doing it your way. Then you won't have to convince anyone of anything."

"That would be much better." Shulamit sighed with relief. "Hopefully I'll find someone selling lamb or vegetables."

"We'd better get back on the road, then, or most of the vendors will pack up for the night before we get there."

They passed the rest of their riding time that day singing, sometimes teaching each other new songs, sometimes singing ones they both knew in two-part harmony. Shulamit's voice was a pretty soprano, but she couldn't project very well; Rivka had a bellowing alto that was startling compared with her gruff, throaty "Riv" voice intended to imitate a male.

The women were still singing when they reached the gates to the town. Rivka pulled on the reins of the horse to pause her so she could tie the cloth mask around her face again. "Queenling, you should probably also be disguised. We attract less trouble if we attract less attention."

"I guess you know best," said Shulamit. She removed the filmy, decorative scarf from her neck and repositioned it as a head

19

covering, wrapping it back around her neck when her black braids were hidden and her face in shadow.

The marketplace was a colorful paradise of food, flowers, and useful household objects. Brightly colored fruits and vegetables spilled out of woven baskets, and in one stall shoppers could buy a different kind of olive for every day of the week. There were also people selling honey or cheese, and a boy talking to everyone who would listen about the scarves his very pregnant mother, sitting in the shade at the back of the stall fanning herself and drinking out of a coconut, had hand-painted in hues of sunset and dusk.

A young man with bushy hair hovered at one of the stalls, examining several different piles of vegetables. He was carrying a large basket, and Shulamit watched him work out some sort of deal with the farmer behind the table. He walked away with the basket filled to the brim with stalks of kohl sprouts. From the quantity, Shulamit guessed it must be for a restaurant, and her mind drifted to a conversation she'd had ages ago, with Aviva.

"You went to the market yourself?" Shulamit had arrived at Aviva's kitchen house to find the buxom cook unpacking a basket full of unusual delicacies. "Why didn't you just send one of the kitchen servants like the head cook does?"

"What, with some list I got out of my head?" Aviva retrieved a strange vegetable from her basket. "How would I ever know what was new, or fresh, or get any ideas? Same old clothes is not what I'm good at."

"What is that?" Shulamit studied the unfamiliar item. It looked like a fluorescent-green cauliflower, but instead of florets, each section rose into perfectly mathematical spiraling peaks. She was transfixed by its beauty and stood there staring, almost in disbelief that such a thing had grown naturally instead of sculpted by human hands — let alone intended for eating!

"I don't know, but we'd never have the chance to find out if I wasn't the type to go to market on my own."

The memory was so vivid that for a moment she almost felt as though Aviva was there with her, but the feeling faded quickly. Swallowing her loneliness, Shulamit hopped from stall to stall, peering inside at the cooks preparing their victuals. Of course, the most convenient takeaway food would have been anything in a pita, but that door was closed forever — or opened into a night of indigestion. She eventually found enough to eat, because the man selling lamb kabobs didn't have meat other than lamb, and the woman selling rice balls was wrapping them in banana leaves. She also picked up a mango, and then, after thinking about it for a moment, bought a second as well.

❀ • ❀ • ❀

Meanwhile, Rivka kept one eye on Shulamit and the other eye on a display of daggers. Should she buy one for the young queen? Or would it just be a liability, because a weapon in the hands of an untrained innocent can easily be used against her? She realized it would probably be a good idea to start teaching Shulamit weaponless martial arts the next time they were out in the open.

They took a room in the Cross-Eyed Tiger, a wholesome-looking inn near the marketplace. An advertisement on the door bragged about the food, and the rates were reasonable. The story they gave the proprietor was simply that a woman had hired protection for her trip to the holy house, which wasn't untrue.

Rivka put their things in the room and then stopped at the cook's stewpot for a plate of something that looked like overcooked chicken and smelled mediocre at best. She could also tell by looking at it that it was going to be too spicy, so she heaped yogurt onto it until the cook glared at her. As if she cared.

21

Shulamit was sitting and eating her lamb kabobs and other finds from the market, when Rivka appeared with a loaded plate. "I should have done that," Rivka commented. "Look at this." She glared at her food.

"I bought you a mango," said Shulamit brightly, handing her the second mango. Until that moment, she hadn't been entirely sure whether it was Rivka's dessert or her own midnight snack. To her surprise, she was genuinely happy that she had decided to give it to Rivka.

"Thank you, Shula!" Rivka began to attack her plate of strangeness with gusto.

Shulamit's face froze slightly, so Rivka reminded her in a whisper, "I can't call you Queenling here. Too risky."

As if to illustrate her point, a group of drunk men at a nearby table had noticed them and began to heckle. "Hey! How come she's got better food than the rest of us?" shouted one.

"They've got mangoes!"

"What is this swill?"

"I want some of that lamb."

One of the men approached the women's table. "That's not fair. Why did he give you better food than everyone else?"

Shulamit looked up from her plate of food with an expression of deep anger, almost like a threatened animal, but before she could say anything, Rivka leapt to her defense. "She bought it in the market. Fowl makes her ill."

22

"Yeah, well, this food would make anyone ill. Hand it over."

Rivka stood up to her full height, towering over him. "You really don't want to mess with me," she growled at him, fingering the hilt of her sword. "Or I might have to buy you a drink with this steel."

The man's eyes opened into wide circles, and he backed away, stumbling. "My apologies, sir." He went back to his table, and nobody bothered them again.

"A traveling comedian he's expecting, not a warrior," Rivka muttered, going back to her food. Shulamit was looking at her with an expression warm like the firelight that lit the room.

"Riv — thank you."

"Oh, that was nothing! Aren't I your — what did you say — hired muscle?"

"No, I mean — thank you for believing me." She paused. "Back at home, I'm a queen. I used to be a princess. So many people think I made up my food problems to get attention, or that I'm just lying to get everyone to take my preferences more seriously."

"Hey," said Riv through a mouthful of chicken curry, "never underestimate your right to the things you like. You have a right to eat mangoes if you want to. Or chase women."

"I guess you're right," said Shulamit, smiling with half her mouth. She appreciated Rivka's support, but "chase" had made her feel awkward. There was a strong physical component to her longings, true, but she hoped Rivka knew that it went beyond that. She was looking for a woman to love, for the sweet mutual understanding of hearts that share each other's secrets—not just a concubine. "But anyway, I really do get sick if I eat the wrong things, or even the right things prepared the wrong way — near the wrong things, I mean. And I'll get sick whether people believe me or not. Aviva was the first person to believe me — and

23

sometimes I feel like she's the only person. Even though I've finally gotten the palace cooks to serve me food that I can eat safely, they all just think I'm being finicky."

"No wonder you fell in love with her," Rivka observed.

"So why did *you* believe me?"

Rivka smiled thoughtfully. "Because you talk to me like a human being," she said, "and not like I'm just part of the peasant crowd beneath your feet. Because you're not the type of person to play the game you just described. You're interested in me and in my story — I know there are questions you're dying to ask and just haven't worked up the nerve. I see it in your face. It means you see me as a person."

They continued eating in peace, their friendship growing by the firelight like a sprouting plant under the rays of the sun.

Chapter 4: Boots

Shulamit lay in bed, wide awake because she had spent the morning sleeping, her brains slowly cooking from being up and down at the wrong times. She wasn't comfortable in the tiny bed, and moonlight poured in through curtains that were pretty, but too sheer to be of much use. Rivka, surely worn out from riding all day, had fallen asleep within seconds of flopping down onto the other bed, so the queen was all alone in her reveries. She thought of Aviva and ached. She thought of her father and wept a little. She thought of how helpless she had felt earlier when the drunk man had challenged her in the dining area, and she wondered how the inn could possibly have the "most inviting kitchen in all of Ir Ilan" as the sign outside had claimed, if the food was really as bad as he and Rivka both seemed to think.

Wonder, wonder, wonder. Too much light. Too much awake. Nervous energy set in. She peered over at Rivka to make sure she was really sound asleep, but then chided herself — any companion, even a sleeping one, would make it impolite to pet herself to wear herself out. Not that it would work in her current mood. Most likely, she would sob and miss Aviva instead of tiring happily.

If only she could fall asleep.

It seemed as if hours had gone by when she realized there were noises in the hallway. She listened to them for a few minutes, trying to entertain herself and take her mind off *Aviva... Aba... Helpless...* by imagining possible scenarios to cause the noises. Perhaps a party of guests had shown up late. But then why were there noises for a moment, and then nothing, and then more noises, and then nothing again?

In fact, the sound appeared and disappeared with regularity.

Since she wasn't sleeping anyway, she slid out of bed. Wrapping her scarf around her shoulders, more out of modest instinct than cold, she padded quietly to the door and lowered herself to the light pouring from its base. It was set high off the floor, the hallway was illuminated for safety, so with her head against the floor, she could peer out into the hall.

Someone wearing a pair of boots walked out of one of the rooms at the far side of the hallway and shut the door. The boots stood in the hallway for a moment, then hurried to the next room. The door opened. As the person slipped inside the room, Shulamit's heart started pounding heavily, filling her with nauseating dread as when she had first heard of her father's accident. A few minutes later, Boots appeared again, and the behavior repeated.

Shulamit hurried over to Rivka's bed and shook her by the shoulder. "Rivka! Wake up — I think someone's robbing the rooms."

Rivka's chest heaved deeply in the breaths of sleep. She did not wake.

"Riv!" Shulamit hissed, right into her ear. Rivka had an interesting, unfamiliar scent, possibly from running around in armor all day. Then, because nothing else had worked, the queen took Rivka's face in both her hands and shook her head slightly but urgently.

Rivka's eyes remained closed, and her body was still languid. The word "Isaac," escaped from her lips like a piece of ash falling on a campsite after the fire was out.

Shulamit could hear the noises getting closer. She smacked Rivka hard in the chest. "Wake! Up!" *She isn't waking up. And he's going to come in here and—*

Whipping her head around quickly, she scanned the room for ideas. At the edge of the room, there was a heavy wooden box where the proprietors of the inn kept extra bedding.

Gritting her teeth in aggravation, she stomped across the room toward the box and tried to lift it. Yeah, right.

She scurried back to the crack under the door and looked across. The intruder was five doors down. Okay. No more time to waste.

Still on the floor, Shulamit slid herself to the far side of the wooden box. With all her might, with all her righteous anger and all her fear, she pushed, pushed, *pushed* until the box began to slide. Muscles burning, she didn't allow herself to pause until the box completely blocked her door.

The door beside hers opened and closed.

She collapsed on top of the box, racking with silent sobs. *Aba! Aba, protect me.*

Someone tried the door.

It remained shut.

My God is my shepherd; I do not lack. In lush vegetation He does cause me to recline...

Eventually, the intruder gave up and went on to the next room over.

Shulamit was still.

❀ • ❀ • ❀

She woke up the next morning at the sun's first light, cramped and sore, after only a few hours of sleep on top of the wooden box. She tried once again to rouse Rivka, but the warrior was still deeply asleep. There was a lot of chatter outside in the hallway, so she felt safe removing the box from the door once she had dressed so that she could venture outside. It took twice as long because she had calmed down, but since there was no immediate threat this time that didn't matter.

The guests of the inn were milling about like ants out of a kicked pile of sand, and many of them looked angry or sad. Here and there she caught phrases:

"Ten thousand it was worth! And never mind that, it was a gift from my late husband! My *late* husband!"

"—*Never* be able to find another like it."

"How will we pay our bill?"

"He took my earrings!"

"I'm missing fifty. What about you?"

"We should have stayed in that other—"

"I didn't hear a thing!"

"To think I should finally sleep soundly, only to wake up to this."

"I wonder why he left my necklace?"

"Maybe it's not real."

As Shulamit feared, the hotel had been robbed. Nobody had been cleaned out entirely, but the man with the boots had been in and out of every room. Or woman. Meeting Rivka had expanded the possibilities for her, and reminded her that clothing was only clothing, not gender.

She scratched her head thoughtfully, concentrating.

Rivka finally appeared in the common area carrying both women's bags, where everyone had gathered to discuss the crime, when the sun was bright in the sky. "I can't understand what happened," she told Shulamit. "I wake up at dawn. We won't be able to make it to the temple by nightfall. I'm not like this. I don't understand."

"I think I do," the young queen said under her breath. "You remember how spicy dinner was yesterday?"

"Dinner was awful."

"This inn bragged about its food. But what I got from the street vendor was much better."

"Maybe they've got a substitute cook."

"I don't think so," said Shulamit. "I think the cook's the one who robbed everyone. I think the spice in the food was covering up the taste of a sleeping drug."

Rivka's eyes narrowed into angry little slits, and her hands curled. "That *shtik drek*." More northern invective followed.

Shulamit swallowed uncomfortably, not recognizing any of the words, but the tone was unmistakable; Rivka's radiating rage was unsettling her nerves even more. "I had my own food, so I was awake. I saw him creeping around from under the door. Well, I saw a pair of boots, anyway."

"You were *awake*? When he came in our room? What did he take? Were you pretending to be asleep?"

Shulamit blinked. "Actually, I blocked the door with that big wooden box."

Rivka lifted an eyebrow, clearly impressed.

"You wouldn't wake up! I was scared!"

"If he came in the room and found you awake he might have killed you," Rivka observed. "Everyone else in the inn was

29

asleep, and cooks have knives. Plus, you don't know how to defend yourself. I was going to talk to you about fixing that."

"You there! Stop talking." The innkeeper called out to them. They quickly straightened up and ended the conversation. "We're going to search everyone," he informed the grumpy guests, "because I locked the door last night and only just unlocked it this morning to receive the milk delivery from the goat girl."

"You could have stolen everything yourself and given it to the goat girl! She's your accomplice!" called out one of the guests.

"No, I saw the transaction," said another guest. "He gave her two coins, and she gave him two bottles."

"I saw too."

"I hope we've settled *that*," growled the innkeeper. "The search begins now."

"They're going to find your breasts," said Shulamit under her breath.

"Shut up," Rivka barked.

It turned out that too many bulky things had been stolen for a search that thorough, but both women still breathed a sigh of relief when they had passed the innkeeper's seal of approval. They watched intently while the cook was searched, but nothing was found on him either.

"Are you done yet?" the cook bellyached. "I have to get back to breakfast. Some of us have *honest* work to do around here, you know.

Shulamit's eyes flew open wide. "Rivka!" she whispered furiously to her companion, forgetting to use the male name in her excitement. "He hid everything at the bottom of the cauldron. It's a perfect hiding place for metal goods!"

Without another thought, Rivka stomped across the room to the enormous stewpot and crashed its contents across the floor. Guests fled from the wave of boiling water and undercooked couscous.

And necklaces and earrings and coins bearing pictures of Shulamit's father.

"Yes, *some* of us have honest work," the innkeeper observed with a lifted eyebrow. Two of the guests seized hold of the cook on either side.

"We are *so* done here," growled Rivka. She threw a handful of coins onto the table in front of the innkeeper and stormed off toward the door. Shulamit scurried after her, stifling nervous laughter.

Rivka didn't speak until they were already on the horse and moving again. "We won't make it there by nightfall thanks to that *nudnik*. I can't believe he drugged me. We'll have to camp."

"That's okay," said Shulamit. "What about breakfast?"

"There's dried goat and dried apricots in my bag. Will that work?"

"Probably," said Shulamit. Then she started to giggle. "You were fantastic back there! I'll never forget the sight of that tidal wave of couscous."

"You were pretty fantastic yourself, Queenling," said Rivka, calming down maybe five percent. "The way you worked out what had happened — you're like a little detective!"

Shulamit grinned. She felt her father would be proud of her that day.

Then her eyes widened again and blinked rapidly. "Rivka, if the robber *had* come into the room and found me awake and killed me, I bet I'd have been in the couscous too!"

"Talk about wheat intolerance."

Even the horse seemed to laugh at that one.

Chapter 5: The Temple

"Sorry today's been a bit of a failure."

"Please," asserted Shulamit, leaning all the way back in the water to submerge her head down to the hairline. "We caught a criminal this morning, didn't get killed, put a few miles behind us, and now we're bathing in this beautiful creek. If this is a failure, I'm looking forward to more of them."

Rivka scrubbed her face vigorously with both hands. "*You* caught a criminal. I overslept because I got drugged by some *putzveytig* who made us late. And now what does the sun do? Shines hotter than usual, and we're stuck here, getting even later."

"But can't we just ride the dragon? Flying is faster than walking, isn't it?" Shulamit felt awkward around a naked Rivka and was keeping to herself near the trees at the shoreline.

"We were already supposed to be flying," Rivka admitted. "That's why I let her rest yesterday, when all we did was walk. Oh, well."

"It's okay," Shulamit reassured her. "We'll still get there tomorrow." She squeezed the water out of her long, thick black hair. "Is her ability to turn into a dragon the reason she's so big?"

"I guess so," said Rivka. "And it's a good thing, too, or else she wouldn't be able to carry both of us."

"Are there many dragon-horses in the north? I've read about your country and heard stories, but I don't remember anything like that."

"Neither had I," said Rivka. "I don't know who bred her. To be honest, I stole her. She belonged to my enemies. But she's been steadfastly loyal to me, so maybe they mistreated her."

33

Shulamit gazed out onto the bank of the creek, where Dragon was grazing peacefully underneath a date palm. She was a large, beautiful, muscled creature, with no signs of her hidden powers save for her size. Somehow, her enormity felt appropriate because her mistress was herself so much larger than Shulamit and her people, so the queen hadn't even questioned it. "So you won her in battle?"

"It's a little more complicated than that." Rivka dunked her entire head in the creek, then whipped it out again, her wet yellow hair flinging water everywhere wildly. "My family's always been at war with another family for control of our little valley. They attacked us, and we — despite what my uncle wanted we should believe — attacked them. I took Dragon from them one night as they tried to storm our castle. Without her help I probably wouldn't have lived."

Still shy of beholding Rivka's apparently unselfconscious nudity, Shulamit looked away, wondering about the granite tone that had come into Rivka's voice. "That sounds terrifying."

"It was the worst night of my life," said Rivka. "And I'm done talking about it right now." Her voice had gone grave.

"Sorry," Shulamit said hastily, mentally groping around for another topic. The name Isaac flashed into her mind, a remnant of the previous night's horrors, and she wondered if he — or his death — had anything to do with the painful topic. She was too scared of upsetting Rivka to ask. "How long have you been a warrior on the road?"

"Two years," said Rivka, "during which I fought in three wars, rescued some people, captured some criminals, and served as temporary bodyguard where need be."

"Where did you learn to fight?"

"I spent a year as the gatekeeper in a bawdy house, if you can believe it," said Rivka with a smirk. "Every time a warrior passed

34

through its doors, I paid him to teach me a new skill, or give me sparring practice."

Shulamit giggled in evidence of her young years. "I don't know whether to wish I was you or not!"

"We're about to introduce you to a whole temple full of women, so how about not," said Rivka. "Although while we're on the subject, you could stand to learn to defend yourself. One never knows. And think of last night."

"But I'm small."

"That doesn't mean anything. There are fighting techniques, used for defense, where agility and a clear head mean more than brute strength. I'll teach you, if you let me."

Shulamit froze. Rivka was still naked, and she would not — *not!* — let herself peek. "You don't mean right now, do you?"

"Of course not. It's far too hot. Unless you want a demonstration here in the water—"

"*No!* I mean — oh, dear." She fidgeted. "Thank you for offering. Maybe at the campsite tonight?"

"It's a deal."

Despite their best intentions, further aggravations plagued their journey that day. Deep into the afternoon, thunder opened up the sky and turned the ground into a sea of mud. The women huddled together atop the horse under the pelting rain. "It's not the safest way, but we have to fly," Rivka told her. "It's the only chance we have of reaching dry ground by nightfall."

"Whatever you think is best!"

The horse transformed and carried the women into the splashing sky. The deep-green wings beat valiantly against the wind, and both Rivka and Shulamit cheered her each time she refused to let the powerful gusts carry her off course. Twice, lightning split the sky and Shulamit yelped after each.

The most terrifying moment, however, was when the dragon's strength began to flag. "She's flying lower!" Shulamit cried frantically.

"Come on, Dragon," Rivka urged. "See that rocky ground over there? That's all. That's all. Good girl." She petted the deep green-black scales.

With renewed energy, Dragon gave it a final push. As soon as they reached solid ground, she landed and almost instantly turned — no,*collapsed* — back into her horse form. "Good girl," Rivka repeated. "Come on, let's get down and let her rest."

After a good long rest, during which the rain thankfully died down, Rivka and Shulamit walked beside the horse down a rocky path. They were still some distance from the temple, but there was no reason they couldn't keep walking until nightfall. Besides, Rivka had mentioned they might find an area where it hadn't rained, so they they'd have firewood for their camp.

That night, as promised, Rivka showed Shulamit a few self-defense basics. In the glow of the campfire they eventually succeeded in lighting, Shulamit practiced throwing Rivka's closed fists off her wrists by twisting her arms in a spiral. "Another thing you need to remember," said Rivka, "is not to let your feelings about your attacker interfere with your defense."

"You mean, if I like the person, and he tries to hurt me, I might not defend myself as well?"

Rivka nodded. "Not only that — another thing that could happen is that you hate him so much that it takes your focus away from your performance."

"Oh, okay, good point."

The lesson was a hard workout, and between its vigors and the trials of the day, both women were ready for sleep before long. Shulamit's mind was as full of reveries as her belly was full of dried meat and dried fruit, and she lay there imagining the future.

After all, tomorrow they would meet the holy women. Though there was no guarantee that any of them would be the husband-fleeing lover of her own sex who Shulamit sought, she still anticipated with great relish the idea of being around such virtuous and mysterious women for a few days. She thought lots of different types of women were beautiful, but it was a *good* woman she sought above all other concerns. Aviva was fragrant and adventurous and made her laugh with her odd pronouncements, but at the core, it was her warmth and kindness Shulamit missed most. Sometimes the ladies-in-waiting treated her as if she were a curiosity, their friendship singed with amusement. Aviva never laughed at her unless Shulamit was already laughing at herself, and she had seemed genuinely interested in what she was talking about instead of listening politely because she was royal.

Shulamit was sure a diverse flock of personalities would inhabit the temple, but beneath their differences, all the women there must have that same inner goodness. Nobody could make their kind of sacrifice without it. She imagined a beautiful sea of mango-colored robes, dyed with turmeric, cloaking delicate, graceful movements and crowned with smiling faces. Maybe they would welcome her with flowers. She had brought a donation for the temple, at any rate. She might be there on extremely frivolous business, but she was still their queen and wanted to do the right thing.

She glanced over at Rivka and noticed the muscles in her face were twitching in her sleep. The last thought Shulamit remembered before succumbing to slumber was to remember the name she'd heard Rivka murmur the night before, and she wondered if Rivka was once again dreaming about her past.

The morning to which they awoke was white and silent. The sky was bleached of all color like forgotten bones, and there was no wind to rustle the leaves around them. Rivka packed up the camp without speaking, while Shulamit fussed obsessively over the braided knots at the back of her head, undoing them and redoing them one after the other several times. Finally, they headed off down the road toward the temple, Shulamit growing more nervous with each footfall of the horse beneath them. She really, *really* wanted to make a good impression.

When they got to the temple, they hopped down from the horse, and Shulamit turned to her companion. "How do I look?"

Rivka smiled. "You look great. Don't be nervous. Confidence is attractive."

Shulamit grinned. "In that case, onward!"

They led the horse inside the temple gates.

Under the white sky, Shulamit beheld the stillness of the courtyard. A dragonfly landing on a small pool of water on the ground attracted their attention simply because it was the only moving thing in sight. The rest of the courtyard was dominated by somewhere between a dozen and two dozen life-sized statues of women in the simple robes of holy women.

Rivka and Shulamit left the horse by the entrance and walked down the central path, looking at the statues. There was something terrifying about them — they were incredibly realistic, and were completely free of dirt, dust, or animal leavings, as if they had just been installed before the women's arrival. Each one was different, and they seemed to be placed haphazardly around the yard.

"Why are their faces so..." Shulamit asked in a hushed voice.

"This one looks like she's had the life scared out of her. What a thing to carve," Rivka commented.

"This one looks angry. I'm scared of *her*!"

"Their poses look so natural, so — lifelike." Rivka furrowed her brow. "I don't understand. I thought you said there's no art in holy houses."

"Something like this would distract from their meditation and simplicity," agreed Shulamit. "And no holy house could afford statuary this well-crafted."

"Don't you dare tell me the holy women carved these," said Rivka. "I won't believe it. Not with expressions like these."

For every single stone face was wracked with pain. In some, it was the pain of anger, of rage, and one statue even looked as if it were ready to attack any observer. In some, it was terror, and in some, merely sadness. Some of the faces were older, and some more youthful.

Shulamit had paused beside a younger face that was shaped in an expression of sad resignation. "She's so beautiful," she murmured, reaching out to gently caress the stone shoulder.

"I don't like it," said Rivka, turning away. "Ho! Who's there?"

An aged woman had appeared from inside the temple, her yellow-orange robe hanging from her frail, bony body as if it had blown into a tree branch during the previous afternoon's storm. "Peace, my son. Peace, my daughter."

"Peace to you," said Rivka and Shulamit together, and bowed their heads in respect.

"I've prayed for your arrival for many months," said the woman. "I'm all alone here and couldn't go for help."

"Help? Why? What's happened here?" Rivka's hand flew to her sword hilt instinctively.

"Please, sit down and have tea with me, my son," she replied. "I'll explain everything. You *must* help us. We have nobody, and we have no money. But you have been sent by God." She turned around and led them inside the temple with faltering steps.

"I hope this isn't a trap," Shulamit whispered as they followed.

"Shhh." Rivka nodded toward her waist, indicating her sword. Shulamit knew that even if it was a trap, Rivka had everything under control.

They sat on simple cushions facing the old woman and let her serve them tea, and then listened as they drank.

"My name is Tamar. I'm the oldest woman here. That is why I'm the only one who wasn't turned to stone when the sorcerer came to steal a wife."

Rivka spewed tea and rocked forward. "*What?!*"

Shulamit covered her face with her hands. "Oh, dear Lord."

"How long ago was this?" Rivka asked.

"I've lost the days, my son," said Tamar sadly. "I'm old and brittle, and I do what I can, but it's not much, not anymore. Each day I tend my sisters. I brush the dirt from their bodies, and sing to them, and tell them I love them. I clean away anything the animals have left, and I pray to God that someone will come and deliver us before age takes me and they're left untended and stone forever."

"You said there was a sorcerer?"

"Yes, my son. He came to us in the guise of a rabbi, but once he was inside, he tried to seduce my sisters. When he realized that none of us would break our vow of celibacy, he got very angry and regained his true form. In the courtyard during our morning prayers he asked us one by one, one last time, if we'd be the woman who would come to him, and we all refused. His anger

40

has been our curse these many days. I alone was spared, because he had no interest in one so old. I thank God for my age, for it has kept me safe to see to their care."

"That sounds absolutely terrifying," said Shulamit. "Those poor women!"

The old woman took her by the hands. "And that's why you must help us, my child. That's why you're here."

"How can we right this wrong?" Rivka's brow was deeply furrowed, her stare intense.

"Go to the sorcerer," said Sister Tamar. "Go to him, and fight him, and win the elixir that blights all curses. I'll show you the way on the map. Only then will my sisters be free, and safe, for I'm failing... my son, I'm failing."

Rivka looked down at her tea thoughtfully. "I'm in the hire of the queen. I can't make my own decisions while on her coin."

"But we have no time," Tamar pleaded. "I have few days. I don't know how many, but once I'm gone, they'll be forgotten and lost and uncared for. We're isolated, and nobody comes here by accident — they'll never be found. Surely she'll have compassion if you were to undertake this task and then beg her forgiveness afterwards. She'll understand."

"Ask her yourself."

"Ask her?"

Rivka turned toward Shulamit, who nodded slightly.

Tamar's eyes grew wide. "Your Majesty! I didn't know! Forgive me for offering only my humble tea, but it's all I have."

"Then it's all I need," Shulamit reassured her. "Riv, can't we rescue the holy women?"

41

"It's your decision, Your Majesty," said Rivka, growing more formal since they were now around another person who knew Shulamit's rank.

"But how could we leave them?!"

"It'll be dangerous. It won't be anything like traveling around visiting temples," said Rivka. "You'll get a taste of my real life, which doesn't usually include queens and pretty lilac scarves made of silk."

Shulamit also understood the words she wasn't saying, which was *This part of the adventure is probably not going to include finding you a sweetheart.* "I know. We don't have a choice. We came here, and now we're the only ones who can fix this mess."

Rivka smiled so broadly it was obvious even though the lower half of her face was covered in cloth. She held out her hand to Tamar. "Then we have ourselves a pledge. We'll start right away."

Chapter 6: Preparations

"Starting right away" meant from that moment forward they would be in the service of Sister Tamar, not that they finished their tea and immediately hopped onboard Dragon. Rivka had lots of questions to ask about the sorcerer before they set out. She followed Tamar as the old woman toddled around the garden, meticulously polishing each of her stone sisters with a cloth.

Shulamit followed them outside and heard her asking about the sorcerer's appearance, about his manner of speaking and his behavior, about his seduction techniques, about whether he raised his voice or became very quiet when angered, and anything else that came up. "I have to know everything you can tell me about him before I meet him in combat," Rivka explained.

"Of course, my son," said Tamar.

Rivka took one of the cloths from Tamar's bucket of water and helped her polish the statues as she listened to the old woman's stories. Altogether, they made a shocking tale of a group of kind, trusting souls betrayed by a manipulative liar. He had tried a different approach with each woman, waiting until he had gotten to know the diverse personalities of the cloister and then tailoring his words and behavior to the occasion. He'd started with the most vulnerable — the youngest and those who still felt some ambivalence about their vows.

"With some of us," said Tamar, shaking her finger knowingly and pausing in her work, "he thought we might already have talked about him. He started right off the mark with a little fiction about how he was a hunted man for a reputation he didn't deserve. He wanted to make sure that if any of us told the others what he had tried, that she wouldn't be believed."

"Such a *mensch*, he's not," said Rivka dryly.

"We were very unfortunate," Tamar agreed. "Excuse me, my son. I have to go have a little private moment. I'll return."

"You're so thorough," Shulamit observed once they were alone. "I'm impressed!"

"Well, I do need to know all of this," said Rivka, "and later on we need to go look at some maps so we'll know how to get to the sorcerer's hold in the mountains. But I'm also hanging around because I wanted to help her, and doing it while we talk saves her dignity."

By the time Tamar had come back, Shulamit had found a third cloth and was vigorously cleaning statues too.

She came to the beautiful, sad-faced novice she'd noted earlier. Tenderly she wiped swaths of water across the statue's feet and wondered if the woman trapped inside could feel it, or sense her in any other way. "I don't know who you are," she whispered, "but if there's any way I can bring you comfort in there, I'll try."

Shulamit's hands were slower and gentler on this one than on the others, and she couldn't help wondering what the woman was like. Had she come here out of deep religious conviction and a desire to serve her fellow humans? Or was she living within these walls in order to hide from the outside world? Did she like to read, and if so, did she prefer stories or lessons? With a rush of heat to her cheeks, Shulamit realized she couldn't bring herself to polish the woman's entire body — not her bosom. She knew she would enjoy it and couldn't live with the guilt of reveling in such a moment at someone else's expense. Especially if the woman was awake inside the stone. "Riv?"

"Your Majesty?"

"We're switching."

Rivka lifted an eyebrow, and the corner of her mouth twitched up knowingly. Shulamit crossed the garden and began to work on another statue.

❀ • ❀ • ❀

Later on, they pored over maps together. "Up there — in those mountains." Tamar pointed on the parchment.

Rivka squinted. The map was blurry and old. "How can you know that for sure? He was a liar, and you couldn't believe anything else that he said."

"Oh, once we all knew what he was doing, we finally figured out who he was. He's quite notorious around here ever since he first showed up from who knows where, two or three years ago... or was it... Anyway, they call him the bird-master. He raises birds, but his real hobby is causing trouble with women. We didn't know that's who the rabbi was. You see, he had changed his hairstyle and put on the right clothing... And he brought no birds with him, so how were we to know?"

She left to fetch a candle, for the sun was departing.

"Will Dragon be able to fly up all that way?"

"I hope so — she should be," said Rivka. "I've let her rest nearly all of today, and that makes a lot of difference. She'll have more than just flying up to the mountains to worry about. The ground on the way there is far too rocky and uneven for a horse. And in between us and the mountain are this lake"— she pointed to the map — "this waterfall"— moving her hand again — "and this other... rock... thing. I'm not taking a horse in that. We fly."

"I'm looking forward to flying when it's not pouring rain!"

45

Rivka grinned. "I'll show you some tricks while we're on our way. We have work to do, though. I'm not tossing you into this without more self-defense training."

"I'm grateful for it."

When the old woman came back, an issue arose over where they would sleep. She refused to let "Riv" sleep in the temple — for no man, even a holy man, was permitted to sleep there. The sorcerer posing as a rabbi had even camped in the courtyard where his victims now stood in breathless sleep. And Shulamit refused to sleep in the temple without Rivka's protection.

"There's always the garden, I suppose," suggested Tamar.

A pebble landed on the ground beside them, and all three women looked up into the dusk. Dragon was standing on the roof, in her horse form, and had kicked it down.

"We could sleep up there," Shulamit suggested. "Then we wouldn't be disturbing all the holy women."

"An excellent solution," said Tamar. "Come, I'll show you the way to the staircase and bring you bedding."

The roof of the temple was a flat surface dominated in the front by a large shallow basin. "Holy water," Tamar indicated.

"Rainwater pools here," Shulamit explained under her breath, no doubt noting Rivka's confused expression, "and the sisters come and bless it. It's a cache that protects the temple."

"Don't drink from it," Tamar warned them. "Now, good night, my son, Your Majesty." She nodded to both of them and walked slowly and carefully back down the staircase to her cell.

"Why didn't she ask how the horse got up on the roof?"

Rivka shrugged. "Age? Or maybe she's so enlightened that she's learned that the world is a much stranger place than most of us realize."

She unpacked some of their bedding, then noticed Dragon had transformed into her reptilian form. "You know what, Shula? You can use as much of the bedding as you want. I'm going to sleep against Dragon."

"Really? That doesn't look very comfortable."

"It's what I'm used to when fighting's on the agenda. It'll help me to wake up as a warrior."

Shulamit nodded. "But won't staying a dragon sap her strength?"

"It's the flying that does that," said Rivka, "not the form. Sometimes I think she prefers this form, but we attract too much attention with a grounded dragon, and she doesn't like that."

"How can you tell what she's thinking?"

Rivka smiled sadly from one side of her mouth. "When you spend three years with one single creature as your only constant friend, you pick up on things."

❀ • ❀ • ❀

Shulamit lay on the bedding and wrapped her silk wrap around her shoulders as she gazed up at the stars. She was just about to lose herself in reverie, possibly about the young woman down there in the courtyard, when she heard Rivka singing. Her strong voice was now gentle, and she sent the melody placidly out into the night. "Jeweled stars, pearl stars, silver coins in olive jars... glittering deep within the dark, see them flicker, see them spark..."

47

Blood rushed into the queen's cheeks. She joined in, tears spilling down her face. Her voice was choked and sounded like hell, but she sang anyway.

They made it through three verses in duet, during which Shulamit held herself together. Then the earthquakes of sobbing began, the type of crying during which nobody is beautiful. She hugged herself and curled up.

"Aba sang that to me to put me to sleep when I was a child," she whispered into her silk wrap, which was now slimy with tears and saliva.

"May his memory be blessed," said Rivka very quietly.

"I still can't believe it, even though I'm queen and there's a shrine and it's been months. It doesn't feel real. He was supposed to get old. His old nursemaid — she was the one who told me he'd fallen off the elephant. I went to him, and he barely woke; they had him under such strong elixirs to ease his pain. But I knew he could sense me, and when I sang that song back to him, I could see tears in his eyes."

Rivka took Shulamit into her arms and folded the little queen's tear-sodden face against the muscled curve of her shoulder.

Shulamit continued. "The sun was so bright that last day — just completely *pouring* into the room. The servants tried putting up curtains because he was too hot, but they wouldn't stay up. It just glowed whiter and whiter until we had to squint to see, even though we were inside. The light got stronger, and he got weaker — almost like he was becoming part of the sun."

The queen was silent, reliving the moment after the incredible glaring whiteness relaxed its grip on the room, and everyone could see distinct shapes again. Curled up in a tight knot on the floor beside her father's bed, her arms clasped firmly around her knees, she felt someone put a crown on her head. She tipped her head forward and let it slide down into her lap, where she hugged it while sobbing.

Rivka's voice brought her back to the present. "You're a smart young woman. He would be proud of you. I'm sure he was proud of you in life too."

The corners of Shulamit's mouth turned up in a heartbroken little smile. "Yeah, he was... he used to tease me about all the books I was reading and facts I'd rattle off from my lessons, but he meant it in a good way. He'd call me his little Princess Brainy."

"That's cute!" said Rivka. "What was he like? I never met him in person, only saw him from a distance."

"He was so full of energy," said Shulamit, pepping up a little as she went back to a happier past. "So many interests. Did you know he knew how to climb up the side of a sheer rock face?"

"No, I didn't," said Rivka, wide-eyed. "I'm impressed."

"And he could speak four languages, and he'd been everywhere," Shulamit continued. "He didn't sleep as much as the rest of us. Sometimes he'd be busy late at night working on laws or listening to arguments in court cases, and have an entire meal in the middle of the night. If I was still up, I'd keep him company."

"It's good that you could spend so much time together."

Shulamit nodded, shifting positions within Rivka's embrace so she could wipe her face clean. "Everyone around me, when they were mourning him, it was so wonderful to be surrounded by people who were sad about the same thing I was because I wasn't alone, but it was also jarring because they were all talking about him as king, not as a father. When we put his kippah into the museum, everyone was talking about how much money it was worth and the embroidery by some famous artist and how it was a national relic, and all this — but I was just thinking of Shabbat, and seders, and — and it didn't mean any of those things to me. It meant lighting candles. It meant he'd hid the afikomen in the palace for me and joking with his advisors as he waited around for me to find it so he could give me a new book. National treasure? I—" She blinked away new tears, but this time the look on her face was one of indignation.

"Do you have anything of his that you carry around as a memento?" Rivka's hand fidgeted with something beneath her helmet.

Shulamit grinned, that bizarre grin of hers that looked more like a grimace than a real smile. "Well, myself! I look like him. Everybody says so. Especially my eyebrows."

"That's perfect. I know you'll carry on his legacy."

Shulamit leaned her head back down against Rivka's chest. "It hurts *so much*. When does this get better?"

"I wish it did," said Rivka. "Instead, we get used to it. We live around it." She paused. "The olive song's special to me too. The man I loved is with me again when I sing it. Thoughts of him still bring me joy, even though they hurt too. I know that if I'm to live my life with a man at my side, it won't be him. I've met many men as I fought in battles and guarded the rich — valiant men, smart men, good, kind men. But I just never looked on them as a woman looks at a man — I mean, as an ordinary woman who likes men — even though I could see their good qualities. I don't think I'm the type who falls in love very often. A man can be a good match, but that's not enough to make him special to me that way..."

"I know the feeling you're talking about," said Shulamit, her face crinkling as she thought about the way Aviva had filled her with exhilaration just by being in the room. "He must have been wonderful, for a woman as amazing as you to have cared for him so deeply." She pulled away from their hug and stretched her arms.

50

Rivka nestled against the dragon's thick hide and closed her eyes. "We have a long way to go tomorrow. Maybe I'll tell you all about him."

Nearby, Shulamit pulled her lilac wrap more tightly around herself, sliding a small patch of the slippery fabric back and forth between her thumb and fingers. The repetitive motion comforted her, and she forced herself to concentrate on something other than the people she missed. The first thing that came to mind was Dragon, so she pretended that she was an artist and quantified each interesting feature, from her clawed and grasping hands to the horns on top of her head. Once distracted from her grief, she fell asleep quickly, for she was genuinely very tired.

❀ • ❀ • ❀

The next morning, after eating breakfast and bidding Sister Tamar goodbye, the two women set out for the sorcerer's hold. Dragon, who had been waiting outside the temple gates still in her reptile form, soared into a brilliant blue sky that promised better weather than their last day of travels. They sailed over the tropical landscape, banana thickets and palm trees clustered together, bathed in early sunlight.

"Want to try something fun?" Rivka asked.

"Okay," said Shulamit, a little hesitantly.

"Trust me." Rivka, confident in her strength and years of practice, tightened her thighs around the dragon's torso and let go of her with her hands. She grabbed Shulamit's hips, holding her firmly down to the animal's backbone. "Hold your hands out into the air while we fly."

Shulamit let out a raucous peal of pure joy. "It feels like it's me who's flying — my arms are wings!" They passed by a noisy

51

white waterfall, and its mist lightly kissed their cheeks in greeting. "*Woooooo!*"

Eventually, Shulamit put her arms down, and they relaxed into a more conventional riding posture. "Thank you so much. I don't think I've ever been this awake." She craned her head around slightly to look at Rivka, and her grin was broad and sparkling under the bright sun.

"Would you like to hear about the man I loved?" Rivka's voice was gentle and intimate. She was pleased with herself for having made Shulamit so happy after last night's tears. Empathy for their shared affliction had opened up her heart, and she had realized just before going to sleep that Shulamit was the first person in three years with whom she felt the impulse to share her story.

"Yes, I would."

And as they sailed over the rocks and the trees, Rivka unfolded her life before her friend.

Chapter 7: The Brat from the Beet-garden

In a valley of the northern lands, there lived a baron who spent half his time wishing he wasn't at war with the family who ruled over Apple Valley, to their immediate west, and the other half of his time cooking up new ways to start trouble with them. He never noticed the hypocrisy of this because he was the least self-aware person in the valley over which he held title. Or *they* held title — depending on whose side you were on.

Rivka was on his side, although she had little choice in the matter because she had been born there. She wouldn't have been *his* first choice either — her very existence was an embarrassment and a burden. Even had she been conventionally beautiful, delicate and demure, and talented in all the noblewomanly tasks of listening and textile art, she still would remain a living, breathing reminder that his foolish younger sister had allowed herself to be, well, *harvested* by one of the workers who grew the castle's beets and potatoes.

Of course, once the pregnancy was discovered, the worker was quickly dismissed from his position and sent away. The other choice was almost certainly death, for the baron valued nothing so much as his reputation, and if he couldn't keep the women in his own *family* safe, well, then the Apple Valley folks would attack at once, thinking him weak!

He wanted the people in his valley to respect him too, so having the daughter of a nobody running around the castle was already embarrassing enough. On top of that, though, she was also nothing like his own sweet daughters. She was a large and ungraceful thing, rough in her manners, too obviously the child of a field hand, but, unfortunately, also too obviously the child of his sister. She was an inconvenience and a source of aggravation. Her childhood efforts to mimic the soldiers, whose presence was a constant at the castle, filled him with dread of what she would be like as an adult.

Marrying her off became his private obsession, with what little brain he had left over after plotting the demise of the Apple Valley ruling house once and for all. Then she would be gone, and perhaps her shallow, uninteresting mother with her, if he could deftly manage it.

But none of the men who would have been appropriate for a relation of his house ever showed interest in his tall, outspoken, physical niece. And certainly he would have rather hidden her away in a tower forever than let her run off with *somebody else*. Too much damage had been done already by his dolt of a sister, Miriam — known by her intimate family as Mitzi.

Not to mention the Apple Valley ruling house and their persistent raids! True, he sent his own men into their valley on occasion, to show them he still had the might to defend his keep. And yet, they sent wave after wave of troublemakers, determined to ruin the peace.

It was so difficult to be the baron of the valley.

One year, after a particularly bloody set of squabbles between the two valleys, a group of wizards who lived in the surrounding mountains decided to take matters into their own hands. Between their magic and the level of respect their Order commanded with everyone in the nation, they were much more powerful than either the baron or the heads of the other family. They were able to use that power to place one of their own in the court of each valley, to oversee matters there and attempt to subdue the feud at its source. They were not an unwarlike brotherhood, but it insulted their very dignity to see wars being fought over a dispute as old and petty as this one. Let each valley to itself in peace, they thought, and if there were wars to be fought, let them be heroic ones.

Rivka, at this point alarmingly too old to have no marriage prospects, was sitting with her mother in the Great Hall watching the newly arrived wizard verbally spar with her uncle. It was rare for anyone else in the castle to contradict the baron, but even without him opening his mouth, his appearance set him apart and marked him a definite outsider. In a household where the men's hair was grown long and usually tied back, his was cropped short. Their beards were full; his beard and mustache were trimmed down nearly to the point where they looked as if they'd been inked with a brush onto his unusually round face. And, most outlandish of all, he wore a black cassock embroidered with strange dark-green-and-purple designs. The wizard was in his late thirties, close to Rivka's mother's age but certainly younger than her uncle — which did him no favors earning the baron's respect.

"This is never going to work," Mitzi observed under her breath. She was knitting on a piece of fancywork, but her eyes never left the two men arguing in the center of the room. "He already hates being told what to do."

"No man could ever win a battle that way!" the baron exclaimed, slamming his fist upon a nearby table.

"Clearly you don't read," said the wizard, sounding more irritated and insulted than angry. "Some already have, in this century *and* the last."

The calmer the wizard's tone, the more the baron turned red. "I have no use for your folktales. Why should I believe something just because it's been inked onto a parchment by some fool in a cassock? Over what my *vast* experience can tell me? I've been fighting these wars since I was ten years old. You were drinking your mother's milk when I first held a sword!"

"I've held a sword as well, in case nobody told you," said the wizard in a quiet, steely tone. He pushed back the right sleeve of his cassock to show the grisly, twisted snake of a scar that slashed across his palm and curled up the length of his forearm. "When the Marantz blade fell, I didn't stop fighting — I learned to brandish my sword in my left hand. So don't assume wizards know nothing of fighting — or of bravery."

"He also hates wizards," Rivka murmured to her mother. "A wizard telling him what to do—"

"Well, it's just that he disagrees with so many things about them," Mitzi explained indulgently, her tone making it clear that she sympathized with her older brother. "He thinks their devotion to histories and parchments, and their vows of celibacy and service, are all unnatural and self-important. He always says the service makes them look weak, and I agree with him that the celibacy's a bit self-centered — like he says, any woman wooed by a wizard would fall asleep of sheer boredom or die of exasperation."

Rivka had heard these words come out of her uncle's mouth before and indeed was mimicking them along as her mother spoke. "He just doesn't like the fact that their power is so much greater than his," she pointed out.

"Can you blame him?" Her mother was not a complicated creature; she liked living in a castle and having someone else clean her room and feed her, and since it was her brother's power that kept her there, she didn't mind his power-hungry stance at all.

Rivka sighed. "He's going to be exceptionally hard on me while he gets used to this, isn't he?"

"Oh, Rivkeleh! He just wants what's going to make you a happy woman someday. He doesn't want you to end up like your old mammeh, hanging around being useless and having even the lowest scullery maid in the castle know her most intimate business." Mitzi smiled sadly.

"Don't worry, Mammeh, I won't embarrass you that way." Rivka smiled. "If I must marry, I'll marry a warrior, so I can go off and fight at his side."

"Rivka, you can't run around holding sticks as swords anymore. You're a grown woman, and it's going to scare away husbands, not attract them."

"We're at war. We're always at war. Why can't I help fight it?"

56

"Because it's unwomanly, and you wouldn't be any good at it. Here. Work on this." Her mother stood up and placed the unfinished piece of lace in her daughter's lap. "It'll help calm your mind and drive away those unsettling thoughts. Don't worry about defending the hold. The men have it under control."

"—*never* let one of you wizards command my men! Are you *crazy*? Wait, why am I even asking that? Of course you're crazy. You've been inhaling parchment fumes and your—"

"—too many of your own men, your tenants and your most loyal soldiers, die every—"

"—never had a woman, not even allowed to *touch* a woman! I bet when you joined up they even cut—"

"—fought under three kings *after* my vows, so don't you accuse me of—"

Rivka looked at her mother and deadpanned, "Yes, the men have it under control." She picked up the knitting and fiddled with it, making three mistakes without even trying on her first row.

She didn't know how she felt about having the wizard around. She didn't disagree with his ideas, but she *was* a member of the family, even if pretty much all of them were completely alien to her; she felt threatened, like an animal whose burrow had been breached.

On the other hand, he had parchments, and some of them were about military strategy or the history of warfare. She yearned to read them. Here, at last, she would find the information for which she had been so thirsty all her life. Caught between her sex and her uncle's distaste for written histories, it had been dry pickings. She had listened intently every time a soldier told a tale, but they presented only the narrowest view, and she knew she needed more.

The idea came into her head that she might get her hands on these parchments in secret and read them quickly, replacing each one before he might miss it. What a delicious prank!

She plotted this for days before actually beginning the project. Already practicing her strategizing, she took note of any times the wizard could predictably be found in the Great Hall (and nearly as predictably, arguing with her uncle over any topic from whether the sky was blue to the treatment of the guard's dogs.) After a while it became apparent that he always lingered after luncheon, usually by falling prey to verbal taunts given out by the baron between the soup and the rest of the meal.

This, then, would be her time of opportunity. She ate her food quickly and unobtrusively, and then, as the baron's voice grew louder and louder in an attempt to drown out the wizard's gentle basso, she slipped out of the Great Hall into the dark passageways.

The wizard had been given a room high in a tower, at the end of two flights of rickety stone stairs. It was actually the room where Mitzi had stayed during the final few months of her pregnancy, hidden away in her shame from curious eyes, and so it was lavishly furnished and relatively clean. But it was as inconvenient a room as the baron could muster, and he was doing everything he could to make it clear that he resented everything about the wizards stepping in and mucking around with his business.

Rivka scurried up the stairs as quickly as was prudent on their uncertain surface and then pushed open the door in one sweeping gesture — better to find out right away if there was some kind of spell put on the room, trapping her or informing the wizard of her intrusion.

Nothing happened.

She looked around the room. It was as she had always known it from her childhood wanderings, save for a few spare cassocks and several trunks, all of which belonged to the wizard. Two of the trunks were open, both containing piles of bound parchments. She stared for a moment, breathing heavily over the sudden wealth at her fingertips. Where to start?

Stepping over to the first trunk and peering in, she read the title of the book on the top. *A Complete History of King Pampas IV's Battles — His Victories and Defeats*. She had no idea who King Pampas was, let alone his three ancestors before him, but she figured this was as good a place to start as any.

Her hand darted out and snatched the book off the pile.

The ceiling did not collapse, and neither did the spare cassocks hanging across the back of the chair get up and block her way. Everything was as it was before. "That's right... He thinks we don't read," she said out loud to herself. *He'd be mostly right*, she added internally.

She was back in her room reading the brittle old book before she let herself relax — not that she could relax completely. Her heart was pounding pretty strongly as a result of her little pilfering adventure. The book in her hands was a connection to all her dreams for the future, and it was a few minutes before she could focus on its words instead of the importance of the moment.

The king in the book had been a great general who lived in another land several hundred years ago. During his reign he protected his people from numerous invasions and also won a civil war when another member of the royal family grew strong against him. She could tell there were plenty of things in the book that could help her uncle, whose situation was always on her mind because it was on his. But she knew he'd never want to hear about anything that had happened to people so irrelevant to his life.

That was okay. She'd find a way to defend his keep even over his own objections.

When she had finished the book several days later, she waited until the daily lunchtime battle and then snuck back into the tower to switch it out for the next one. So did Rivka bat Miriam slowly make her way through the books in the trunk. Her hungry mind soaked up all the new information. She didn't dare take notes for fear they'd be found, so while she ran around in the garden feeling the sun's warmth battle the crispness of the air, or during bad weather when she was trapped inside mangling yet another piece of fancywork, she repeated the important points to herself over and over until they were nearly as automatic as *Bless you, O Lord, King of the Universe...*

One day, she had taken one of the books into the garden because she knew a place in a tree where she wouldn't easily be seen and could hide there to read in peace. She opened the book, and to her breathless horror she beheld an unfamiliar scrawl—

If you're going to borrow my parchments, why not ask permission?

Chapter 8: The Wizard

Rivka's first reaction to the note was, naturally, to panic about being caught, but then the warrior's heart that could not be squashed within her neither by motherly concern nor avuncular edict woke up and wrote back her response.

Only to have you say no?

She didn't give the wizard any especial look of deference that evening, nor did she return the book until she was good and finished with it. Then, and no sooner, she returned to the tower and exchanged it for the next one in the pile.

His reply was waiting for her two books later. *And have me say yes. Anyone in this dank monument to human ignorance who finds value in these histories would be a welcome friend.*

After that, she felt as though they had a secret inside joke. She supposed that eventually the joke would be on her, because he never guessed that she was female. She was sure this was why he let her write about her dreams of becoming a great warrior and helping to defend the keep, and encouraged her instead of trying to silence her like everybody else. If he ever found out, she presumed, he'd probably gently but firmly admonish her for her presumptuous plans.

How are you with a sword?

I look forward to my opportunity to find out.

If you're able, I'll give you instruction. I would find it a welcome respite from what I endure in the Great Hall, wrote the wizard back in brazen disrespect of the baron. He surely knew full well that a book in the bottom of an old trunk would never find its way into the baron's hands even by accident. Especially not the *middle* of a book.

Rivka wished he could give her lessons via notes scribbled in books, but that was probably impossible. Besides, she had no sword. Not even a broken remnant from a heroic father lost in battle. Instead, he had left for her the nickname Rivka bat Beetgreens, daughter of the vegetable garden, as if Mitzi had gone out walking one night and been defiled by the crop itself.

I would gladly learn if I could, she wrote back into the book, *but if I can't, what are the first things I should know?*

When she was finished with lunch, she tried to leave to return the book, but her mother kept her a few minutes just outside the Great Hall asking if she thought this or that new piece of jewelry more fine upon her ears. She picked one at random, eager to get the book back to the wizard's room before his daily argument with the baron was concluded. No danger of its being over any time soon, she thought — even this far from the Great Hall she could hear her uncle bellowing. Would it hurt him to just *shut up* even for only a few minutes?

Gladly moving away from the sound of his voice, she rushed up to the tower and into the wizard's room. She picked up the next book in the pile, placing the previous one on the stack in its place.

"What's that there?"

Rivka froze.

She turned around to face the wizard, who had been sitting in a chair in the corner of the room. She hadn't seen him in the shadow, and nobody had ever been in the room before when she had come up.

"How are you here? The baron—"

"Is abusing someone else today, blissfully enough for me." He stood up. "You're not what I was expecting. A soldier's page, perhaps, or a stableboy."

62

"Not the baron's bastard niece?" She faced him without fear, daring him to send her away with steady eyes and even breathing — even though her heart was pounding heavily.

The wizard opened one of the trunks that had always been closed and locked during her visits and took from it a long flashing thing of silver steel. He straightened up and approached her, offering her the hilt. "Do you have the next hour free?"

❀ • ❀ • ❀

Far across the fields, there stood an abandoned shell of a barn, four stone walls with nothing but sky overhead. Together, without speaking much, they cleared away the remains of what had been the roof. When there was enough space for them to move, the wizard showed her the basics of swordsmanship. She entered the practice with a lot of zeal and strength, the natural outcomes of her lifelong interest and her athletic temperament, but she was also gravely unpracticed at telling her body what to do.

"We'll work on the swords," he said, after watching her for a time, "but I think I should also show you some exercises to bring you in touch with your movements, and in control of your body."

Rivka concentrated on her lesson and committed everything he told her to memory. At the end of the session, she thanked him profusely and tried to give him back the sword he had lent her.

He held up his hand. "Keep it for now. Someday you'll have your own, but that one's only an extra, a token of appreciation from one of the kings under whom I fought — you can read about it on the inscription — and I barely even use the one I truly consider mine." He held up his own blade, the one in his left hand. "I fight with the wrong hand," he explained. "Had to learn to write with this one too."

63

"I saw your scar," said Rivka.

"Oh, in the Great Hall? Your uncle certainly brings out the warrior in my *tongue*, that's for sure, even if my hands are often idle." He drew back from her. "I think I know where I can find some old rakes nobody will miss. Take off the heads and they'll make good safety weapons. I know you'll practice before then, but you'll have an easier time of it if you start with that."

Rivka nodded enthusiastically. "Yes, of course! I'm so grateful... Wizard...?"

"My name's Isaac," he said.

"Rivka," she said. "But surely you knew that."

"Even if I did, it's new to me now," said the wizard with a smile. "Before today, I knew you, and I knew my strange friend who was stealing my books and returning them after reading them. Now that I know who you are, I meet the name anew."

"I won't let you down," Rivka assured him.

"Let me down? No, Rivka, I don't do this for my own glory. I'm teaching you as an excuse to interact with the one other soul in this cave who values learning and knowledge."

"What book should I read next?"

"Since we've broken out the swords, I'll lend you Face's Treatise on sword craftsmanship. You'll learn about words like 'tang' and start thinking about angles of swing."

"I'm ready for anything."

"I can see that already."

❀ • ❀ • ❀

Rivka had never felt better in her life as she did when she smuggled the sword back to her bedroom and spent all evening after dinner practicing with it. She also remembered to dutifully repeat the weaponless exercises that Isaac thought she needed, and she was pleased to discover that they caused a marked improvement in her carriage and movements over the next few weeks. The slight change in her made her catch the baron's attention, and reminded him of his search to find her a suitably honorable husband.

Rivka and Isaac met whenever they could within the forgotten stone walls. They fought with the wooden rake-handles until she was ready to graduate to full-time sword work. Sometimes he talked about his history in battle, using his own adventures to illustrate lessons in combat. Rivka eagerly soaked up every story, determined to have her own someday.

Of course, it wasn't all easy. Learning how to fall safely meant collecting a full spectrum of bruises before she mastered the technique. Luckily, she already had a reputation for "unladylike" behavior, so the few that showed up in places her dresses didn't cover generated nothing beyond the unbridled disdain of her married cousin, Frayda, the baron's eldest daughter, who was visiting to show off her new baby.

The hardest part came when she had mastered parrying and thrusting, and now faced the step where she must decide which order in which to put them, to keep an enemy on his guard. Rivka, whose brain wasn't wired to constantly plan attacks complex enough to surprise an opponent, practiced incessantly until varying her choice of blow became instinct.

One day, as Rivka and Isaac were sparring in the rain, she realized to her heady surprise that she was besting him in blow after blow, and that all her months of practicing had grown her skill to where she outshone Isaac's uninjured but non-dominant left hand. She continued wielding, not quite understanding the placid, yet slightly impish expression on his round face. What would she do for practice if she could now easily beat any sword he could hold?

His answer came in the form of swirling ribbons of light that suddenly appeared from his right hand. They surprised her and surrounded her sword, but then she roused herself and slashed back at them heavily. Then she put her sword down by her side, blinking raindrops from her eyelashes. "What was that?!"

"I can't close these fingers around the hilt of a sword anymore," Isaac explained, "but I can still do magic." He was usually fairly tight-lipped on exactly what wizard training entailed and didn't reveal more than was necessary.

Rivka didn't move, squinting at his hands critically as she studied the winding silver whips.

"They won't hurt you," Isaac reassured her, sheathing his sword. "You won't even feel them, not in the beginning."

"And then what?"

"An irritating buzz. Enough to sharpen the game. Rivka, mind your sword!" The whips jetted out of both of his hands with no other warning, and she quickly raised her steel to meet them.

❀ • ❀ • ❀

His magical abilities were a perfect grindstone for her skill, because he could improve both the stakes and the complexity of their sparring matches almost infinitely. Over the year that followed, she grew to be a formidable warrior, all under her uncle's nose. Every day when the maid was cleaning her room, Rivka took the sword out from under her bed and hid it behind a suit of armor that stood as decoration in the passageway. It was a

66

terrible hiding place, but it was only there for an hour each day. Thankfully for Rivka, the maid was like clockwork, and this was not difficult — only annoying.

The wedding of Cousin Bina, the baron's middle child, was approaching, and as soon as Rivka heard that the great General Zusmann was on the guest list as a good friend of the groom's, she remembered her plan to marry a warrior and follow him into battle. She showed uncharacteristic interest in her frock and jewelry for the event, filling her mother's face with smiles and her cousins' with mocking eye-rolls. When they had finished with her, she looked passably pretty in dark brown, even though she towered over her cousins. The vegetable gardener had been a tall man, and from that, one could not escape.

She studied her reflection in the glass. Would the general find her appealing? She was greatly interested in anything he had to say about his adventures, or his ideas on various bits and pieces of military theory. She had reread a couple of Isaac's books on strategy before the wedding so she could make sure to follow the general's conversation and show by her replies that she was a worthy wife.

The baron must have had similar ideas about his lowborn niece and the single, respectable general, for he engineered a partnering of the two during one of the row dances in the Great Hall after the wedding ceremony was completed. Rivka did her best to lead his conversation to the field, and he gladly followed her there to relive his past exploits. But when she said, "Certainly a fitting wife for you would be she who could hold her own in battle," his reply dashed her hopes.

"My wife? What an idea!" The general laughed. "My wife needs to stay at home and show the world evidence of that which produces my strength on the field, by breeding my sons."

Rivka couldn't suppress a face of disgust. She got through the rest of the dance somehow, but then fate added to her distemper by pairing her with her uncle for the next dance. "How did you scare him off, you foolish girl?"

"I didn't scare him off. He scared *me* off."

"In what way have you found him wanting? He is honorable, powerful, and wealthy."

"He wouldn't let me fight for him, just as you refuse to let me fight for you." Rivka's patience with enduring her uncle's mindset was wearing thin of late, in direct proportion to her confidence as she gained skill at the blade.

"What would the family of Apple Valley think if they saw a woman defending my keep?" The baron snorted derisively. "They'd see a weak old man so desperate and confused he'd send out his own womenfolk in front of him as a shield! They'd attack *tomorrow*, and you wouldn't know what to do. Imagine a woman fighting one of *them*. Huh." He made a noise that reminded her of a barking dog. "You wouldn't know the first thing about fighting."

"I'm done." Ripping through an absolutely unbreakable rule of etiquette, she dropped out of the dance and stormed across the Great Hall to an uninteresting corner in shadow.

The dance continued smoothly as an older woman who had not been dancing rose swiftly to the occasion and filled in the place Rivka had vacated.

Isaac appeared by her side. "Theatrics?"

"He's insufferable," she grumbled.

"Which one?"

"Yes."

"We could spar after the ball."

"Please. I don't think I could sleep very easily after this."

"I'll be there."

"I'll try not to cut off your hands."

Making no comment about the strange things her frustration and rage were making her say, Isaac floated away into the crowd. Rivka's mind was moving a mile a minute, and the ballroom had become an oppressive distraction as she struggled to keep up with her own thoughts. She needed to get someplace quiet, where she could think without being disturbed.

She slipped outside into the crisp night air. Without too much thought about how it would stain or rend her dress, she crawled into the little cavern made by the low-hanging branches of the tree where she had first read Isaac's handwriting in the book.

The general's disdain for her dreams had horrified her. What entrapment he offered her! What an infinitely tall tower of imprisonment! After spending several years naïvely assuming that a man with a sword would want a woman who matched him, she had discovered in one moment how very different that woman was who he expected — the woman into whom he would have tried to change her.

Speaking with Isaac after such an insult had felt like eating the roast chicken after the stale bread. This was the way she wanted a man to talk to her — to be concerned for her feelings, to invite her to spar, to be unafraid of her aggressive moods. Far from being a wet blanket upon her fiery nature — instead, he was a sturdy hearth that nurtured that fire and gave it a safe place to flourish. She was happiest when she was around him and looked forward to their next meeting when they were apart. Often, she wished for his company in unlikely moments.

A frisson of fear rippled through her body. She forbade herself even to think the words. But the idea itself, wordless, bubbled forth from her heart and could not be contained. Try as she did,

69

she couldn't suppress a sudden thought of the thick solidness of his body — tall, strong, and a little stout but sturdy — and his impish, placid expression and pointed eyebrows that suddenly made her think of a cat smiling at you with its eyes closed. She saw them with new eyes and clenched her fists at her sides.

Feeling as if her very blood had been replaced by a substance both unfamiliar and intoxicating, she went to her room to collect her sword, ready to meet him at the battlefield of her heart.

Chapter 9: Press the Night, Collect the Sun

Rivka darted around within the stone walls, each stroke of her sword falling silently on one or two of Isaac's spiraling whips of light. She hated the startling buzz they made if they touched her, and they made a strong but ultimately harmless incentive for her to be on her toes with her technique. After her heart had burst like a ripe grape, exposing unseen parts to her conscious mind, she had been filled with a relentless manic energy, and tonight, she fought off the whips with extra vigor.

The whips didn't catch her at all, and she thought her technique was flawless. But in one swift moment, Isaac once again changed the game. Moving his hands down to his sides, he suddenly looked into her eyes. "You are distracted."

In an echo of her courage in his room in the tower on the first day of their sparring, she faced him without flinching or denying anything. "It's of no consequence," she retorted. "It wouldn't be a factor with any adversary I would meet in battle."

She knew there was so much he was trying to say with his eyes, and with the rest of that impish face, but all he said was, "Ah, but what if you hate him as much as you..." He stopped.

Rivka knew why he was silent. The celibacy vow of the Wizard Order was held in place by a number of strange and terrifying spells, the price of each wizard's entry into the secret magic they taught. If he touched a woman, if he spoke about love to a woman, or even moved his hands in the shape of the letters to write them — she had known this from the beginning. Fool that her heart was, it didn't care.

But she didn't want to scare him away. "I ask nothing of you but the friendship you already give," she blurted out. She could endure her feelings, but what if he found them threatening? Or even insulting?

"I'm not scared of you, Rivka," he said quietly. Then, after a moment of consideration, he lifted his right hand and blasted light at a halved log in the corner. She stood in place, puzzled, until he motioned with his head for her to go look.

She had to bend down and bring the log close to her eyes to read the words that he had branded there in the most beautiful script she had ever seen,

I can give only my heart, but it is absolutely yours.

Her mind stopped, halted in that moment of discovery, and she might have even forgotten to breathe.

"Rivka, mind your sword!" And the next thing she knew she was fumbling to block his attacks again. He aimed one of his hands at the log as they continued to spar, and it burst into flames, destroying the evidence — everywhere but within her breast.

They spoke no more that night of what Rivka now knew to be a mutual love, but now that the egg had been cracked there was no putting it back into the shell. Rivka tossed and turned in her bed, longing to be with him, exploring thoughts she had never before considered. She ran her hand down her body, imagining it was his touch she felt. At the very idea, she cried out into the night.

Sleep would not come. She could think only of him. And so she arose, wrapped her dressing gown around her body, and crept into the passageways.

There was a knock at the wizard's locked door.

"Who disturbs my sleep?" growled a familiar bass voice, the low tones resonating more powerfully and more harshly than usual through the door.

"Please let me in."

"What happened to not asking more of me?"

"I'm sorry — I'm weak—" She pressed herself against his door, yearning for the impossible, wanting him to hold her and turn whatever felt like a heart beating between her legs into an oasis of sweet relief.

"No, you're strong because you know what you want and you're not afraid to ask for it."

"Open the door, I beg of you."

"You know my vows."

"I promise not to shame you. I won't even look at you. I just want to be near you." She banged on the door once with both fists. "I'll stay out here if I have to."

"Heed, Rivka." He was close to the door now, and even this intimacy shot ribbons of feeling through her body. "Go back to your room and close your door, and if you promise not to open it during the night, *I* promise that I will follow you and stay with you on the outside as you sleep."

"Why my door, and not yours?"

"Because I would rather the risk of being caught in the passageway fall to me. Let this be something I can give you."

Breaking, Rivka whispered, "I promise!" and made for her room as quickly as she could.

Shutting the door behind her, she remained right beside it, eventually sitting on the floor with her back against the door as she waited. Finally, she heard his voice. "Rivka."

"Isaac," she replied, her face spreading into a grin. "I'm sorry—"

"You have no reason to apologize," he said. "My vows are mine alone to keep — my burden and my responsibility — not yours. Cherish your feelings, and don't be ashamed of them. Enjoy them as I cannot."

73

"Then I love you, and in my mind you're holding me."

He began to sing in another language. It was the speech of Perach, to the south, just as in their prayers, but the text was one she'd never heard before.

Jeweled stars, pearl stars
Silver coins in olive jars
Glittering deep within the dark
See them flicker, see them spark
Press the olives, pool the oil
Golden sunlight, golden royal
Press so olive oil will run
Press the night, collect the sun...

She leaned into the door and let his deep voice resonate through her body, caressing her with sound. As he sang, delight flooded her brain and drove out all thought.

For several hours they shared hearts, talking of their childhoods and of his adventures out on the battlefield. As sleep finally overtook the frustrated but soothed maiden, she said to him, "I hope that I dream that we're fighting side by side." It wasn't all she was hoping to dream, but what she'd said out loud had a reasonable chance of coming true — at least, in the alternate reality where the baron would let her fight and would respect Isaac enough to take his advice. And she didn't want to make him feel guilty for holding true to his vows, which he couldn't break even if he wanted to without serious wizard consequences.

"I hope your dreams bring you comfort," was his heavy-laden reply.

She hugged herself and felt his love in it. He sang again until she slept.

❀ • ❀ • ❀

Two days later, the maid was sick. Somebody else cleaned Rivka's room and came at a different time, and before Rivka knew anything about it, the alternate maid had found her sword and shown it to enough people that it was too late to try to bribe anyone to be silent. She rushed toward the Great Hall, hoping to intercept her uncle before someone else told him about the sword. She knew he'd take the secrecy just as badly as the disregard of his wishes.

"Uncle!" She dashed into the room in a hot flurry of skirts. Then she clapped her hands to her face and shrieked.

Isaac was standing in the center of the room, grimacing, with Rivka's sword pointed fixedly at his throat — courtesy of the baron.

Chapter 10: The Blood-Streaked Flower

"Deceit. Deceit, and shame, and insult." With each percussive word, the hand that held the sword twitched slightly, as if the baron were trying very hard not to simply kill the wizard there and then. "You invade my castle with your useless ideas and two-faced words of peace, and then embarrass me before my enemies. Was that your game all along, wizard? Show them that our forces are so pathetic that a bastard wench must raise a sword in our defense? Whose side are you on?"

"She has talent." Isaac's voice was quiet, grim, and resolute.

"A woman *cannot* wield a sword!" the baron bellowed. "You defile my house with your insolent ideas. Hersch!" He gestured to an attendant page. "Fetch a messenger. Then go to my private weapons room and bring me the black box that sits in the southeast corner."

Rivka studied him, looking for an opening, but he had been a lifelong warrior and the hand that held her blade showed no sign of weakness. Instead, she said simply, "Uncle, I *can* fight for you. You and I both know it's useless for me to add that I wish it wasn't true, but the Apple Valley troops are always a danger. I promise that I can help you repel the next attack."

"Useless — your *promise* is *useless*!" screamed the baron, close enough to Isaac's face to cause the stoic, stony mask of anger to momentarily flinch. "You would collapse at what I've seen in one half-minute of ordinary battle."

"Uncle—"

He put up his other hand. "Save your breath. Guards, hold my niece."

Before Rivka could dart out of the way, four strong men appeared from the shadowed corners and grabbed her arms and legs. She wriggled with all her might, but none of her heavy, muscled pushes could break her free. There were simply too many guards.

"Wizard, you have interfered with the supervision of my valley, you have interfered with the peace of my home, and now you have interfered with my family — especially this fatherless girl whose upbringing has been my burden these many years." The baron sounded like a judge passing down a verdict. "Of course her weak woman's mind would believe whatever twaddle you told her about dead kings and theoretical battle plans based on dreams."

"You would dig in a gold mine and see only potatoes," Isaac growled. "And you would swallow them whole, bitterly regretting your misfortune while filling your stomach with countless riches."

"Why, you—"

"I hope you choke on them."

"I have a sword to your throat! Your words mean nothing."

But to Rivka, bound and struggling, they meant everything, especially as one who had been called Daughter of Beet-greens. She knew in her heart, with a certainty as real as the air in her lungs, that Isaac valued her as nobody else had. Beets and potatoes come up from the earth and taste of earth. Gold comes out of the dirt but shines like sunlight.

The messenger entered, followed by the page and his cargo. "Sire, you sent for me?"

"Yes. Report this message to the Wizard Order in the mountains," said the baron officiously. "I've found their wizard representative completely unacceptable and demand his removal immediately. If they insist on replacing him — if they *must* nursemaid me — tell them to send me someone who isn't so

77

insufferably *smug*"— he glared at Isaac — "and who doesn't constantly quote ancient histories, and who won't disobey my rules in my own castle! You never should have even spoken to the girl, fool wizard."

The messenger cleared his throat. "Sire, was that all?"

"What? Oh, yes. Yes. Just tell them to get here as soon as possible to collect him."

"Collect him?" Rivka's heart pounded in her ears.

The baron's response was to gesture at his page for the black box.

Rivka's glance met Isaac's. In that moment of terror she memorized his eyes. For a moment, she was able to forget the room, the sword, the baron, the four strong men holding her, and the nightmare she was sure would follow.

The baron's free hand emerged from the black box holding a small vial of liquid. "Wizard, I don't believe for a moment you would actually leave if I banished you awake. You're a sneaky, slithering, treacherous, interfering—"

"What is that?" Rivka demanded.

"Shut up, girl! It's sleep... sleep in a bottle." He held it up for her. "He's going to drink it, and then he won't be able to cause any more trouble until the other wizards come to get him and *take him far away.*"

Isaac pursed his lips and glanced up at the baron defiantly. He lifted one of his pointed eyebrows and closed his lips tightly.

Rivka noticed his hands at his side, slowly tensing into action. She silently prayed that his magical whips of light would be swift and effective. Could he use them to free himself and get out of the room before the baron could swing his sword?

"Guards, knives," said the baron, unexpectedly.

In one confusing moment, light flared from Isaac's fingers, and the guards holding Rivka suddenly held daggers to her flesh. "You would harm your own blood?" he growled at the baron in horror.

"Of course I wouldn't kill her," explained the baron. "But there are things those men can do with their daggers that I know you don't want them to do to her." He grabbed the wizard's right arm and pulled back his sleeve roughly to expose the scar across his wrist and forearm.

"You monster," Isaac growled. Rivka had never seen him so bitterly angry, almost as if he were buried under an avalanche of his own rage.

"Drink the cordial like a good little irritating meddler," said the baron, "and Rivka won't be harmed."

"*No!*" Her voice was like a hawk's scream.

"Shut *up*, girl!"

"Get those things away from me!" Rivka hissed at the guards. They were trying to be extra threatening by showing her how sharp the daggers were, shaving off bits of hair on her arms. Her fists clenched, and she longed for an army.

"Isaac—"

The wizard looked at her straight on, ignoring the baron completely for a moment. "I believe in you."

Then he tilted his head slightly and opened his lips.

Without taking his eyes off Rivka, he let the baron's rough hands tip the contents of the vial into his mouth.

"No!" Rivka's jaw shook. Everything shook. "I'll find you."

The wizard's blue eyes closed, beholding last an image of tall, blonde Rivka, trembling pridefully in the grasp of her captors. He fell limp into the arms of more guards who had turned up at the baron's gesture.

"No, you won't," said the baron calmly. "Guards, get her into her room and lock the door from the outside. Make sure she gets regular meals."

Stuffing the frantic, fighting Rivka into her room was like trying to bail out a boat that was leaking in fourteen places, but the guards managed it somehow and then bundled themselves off to dinner. She wore herself out banging on the door and then collapsed onto the floor with her hands once again clenched into fists.

She rushed to her window. It was too high to make a practical escape, despite the deep pond just beneath. Studying the landscape just outside the castle, her eye caught movement on the ground. What was that, if not the guards carrying the unconscious wizard into one of the wooden towers that had been built as storage for last year's exceptionally bountiful crops? She stared at the strange, horrifying procession, torturing herself with every moment of beholding Isaac in such a state. He was beautiful in repose — that repose should be with *her*, not as punishment for her friendship!

The guards disappeared with their prisoner into the tower, and before long she saw them in the topmost window, two or three stories up, fussing around in the room. Probably making room for him amid the sacks of beets.

Realizing she wasn't going to be able to watch him anymore — they must have lain him down on the floor — she looked around the room and tried to plan an escape.

Unfortunately, the guards burst in a little while later with her food, interrupting her knotted bedsheet rope scheme. She wasn't quick enough to hide it under the bed in time, and they took it away with them. They left part of a chicken and overcooked kasha varnishkes in its place, but it was a poor trade.

She ate for strength, not pleasure.

❀ • ❀ • ❀

"Rivkeleh."

"Mammeh, isn't there any way you can soften his heart and get me out of here?"

Mitzi sighed through the door. "He's right — you can't keep getting involved in these dangerous things that you don't understand."

"I do understand."

"You say you want to fight. You could get killed out there."

"Has it occurred to you that I might be good enough that I would actually survive a battle?"

"Your uncle has tried to give you all that a woman needs in life — a nice bed to sleep in, good food, pretty clothing, social position — which, need I remind you, you and I are not naturally blessed with, thanks to my behavior at your age."

She still thinks I'm fifteen. "I'm not you, Mammeh. Those are all the things *you* need."

❀ • ❀ • ❀

Several hours later, Rivka had taken up position at the window to gaze out at the tower through the cool night air. There was nothing to watch, but she felt closer to Isaac if she could at least see his prison. So deep was she in her thoughts — of his voice, his unspoken love, his sacrifice — that it was several minutes before she noticed the men on horseback riding into the grounds. She squinted into the inky night, trying to see—

Someone else raised the alarm, and then she realized what was going on. Their enemies from the other valley. What timing! Was her whole life to collapse like a poorly constructed model house of sticks in one climactically awful night?

If only she could get out of the room and help fight. Not that she had her sword anymore, of course. Her uncle had awarded it to Lev, one of the guards who had been shaving the hairs off her arm with his dagger. *Her* sword — that had Isaac's name on it.

Women were rushing around in the passageway screaming, and she heard the heavy clomp of men's boots as they prepared for battle. "Let me out! Let me fight!" she screamed at nobody, and nobody answered.

Hastening back to the window, she saw that a group of attackers holding torches were spreading flames across the land. Reaching her hands out the window at them as if she could hold them back with sheer will, she tried to pray them away from the tower where Isaac lay. "Please," she cried uselessly into the night. "He's asleep. He can't escape. Oh, please!"

It was unlikely the men downstairs had any idea that they were destroying anything beyond resources. The inexorable torches moved toward the tower and kissed it with flame. The structure was constructed out of wood, and caught easily.

"*No!*" Rivka grabbed the sides of the window with both hands and wriggled through, then launched herself from its height into the pond below. She had no room in her heart to fear the fall. All her fear was for that dearest heart trapped high in the burning tower.

She hit the water with a violent splash. When she lifted her head above the surface and wiped the droplets and dripping hair from her face, what she saw by firelight turned her blood to a frozen poison.

The tower...

Rudimentary remainders of the first story were still standing, as black sticks amidst a forest of orange flame. But the upper stories were completely gone. Ash was everywhere. Men ran and horses galloped back and forth, thundering over the quiet rumble-crackle of the fire.

Rivka walked out of the pond, her wet dress not the only shackle weighing her down. She kept her eyes on the ruined tower, unable to ask—

The ash-laden wind whipped up, chilling her and plastering her face with a cloth rag with singed edges that had flown about on its eddies. She pulled it away from her face only to shudder in fright.

It was a piece of Isaac's cassock.

She gasped as if she were breaking, her legs weak and shaky and barely holding her up, and then screamed. A horrible feeling devoured her stomach and threatened to rip the breath from her throat.

Before she had time to think, a warrior wearing the Apple Valley crest approached her on horseback. He made as if to draw his sword, but his unusually large horse, most likely spooked by the fire, suddenly reared and threw him off. With one quick look back at the surprised invader, lying on his backside in the mud, she leapt onto the horse's back. It didn't occur to her that a spooked horse might not like her either.

Once on the horse, she wrapped the cassock fragment around her hair and knotted it. She could shatter into a thousand pieces later for all she cared, but right now, without a way to defend herself, her first idea was to get out of the fray and back into the castle.

She rode away from the confusion at the burning crop towers and toward the castle entrance. The battle had been here already and moved on, and the last few steps of the horse were in between corpses — those of her own family's guards, but also those of invaders from the other valley. They lay here and there all mixed together, all human in death.

The main entrance was still a confusion of swords and shouting, and since she still had no sword, she guided the horse into the relative safety of the shadow made by a side doorway. There, she took a deep breath and looked around her.

A glint of metal on the mud caught her eye.

Lev lay faceup and lifeless, and beside him was Rivka's sword.

Without another thought, she hopped off the horse and grabbed it. For a moment she could do nothing but clutch its hilt with both hands, and then suddenly she broke into bone-quaking sobs. *Isaac*. Never to spar with him again — never to see his face again, hear his voice, all lost—

Focus.

She looked back down at Lev's corpse. His battle armor of leather and metal looked relatively undamaged by the fate that had felled him. After placing the sword against the corner of the doorway for safekeeping, she dragged the body into the shadows and quickly removed every useful bit of battle-kit.

Caring nothing for modesty in that strange night, she cast off her dress and donned the pants, the tunic, and the helmet.

The sword felt perfect in the scabbard she now wore across her waist.

Jumping back onto the back of the enormous mare, she raised her sword and dashed into the thick of the battle.

It wasn't long before she found the baron. He was bravely holding the doorway against three men at once — despite being an awful person he was indeed a good fighter. But eventually a fourth invader fought his way through the lesser guards and tipped the balance.

The baron gritted his teeth and plowed into them, surely knowing that he risked his life.

"Hyahhh!" Rivka shouted, galloping forward on her horse. She helped her uncle to drive back the four men, then fought at his side for the rest of the battle. At one point, she even sliced off an arm that was about to stab the baron in the kidneys. She didn't know whose arm it was, and she didn't have time to care. The warrior spirit Isaac had brought out in her was fully born, and there was no putting the flower back into the bud, that flower that was now streaked deep red with the blood of her enemies.

Nobody had any idea who she was.

When the thing was done, and their enemies had been driven away for the time being, she stalked into the Great Hall where the baron was feeding the survivors thick, awful coffee and an impromptu breakfast of boiled potatoes. "Uncle," she said, breathlessly, removing her helmet. "So you see, I can fight."

The baron's weary but satisfied face twisted into a fiery scowl. "What — that was *you* out there?"

"I saved your life, Uncle." Her smile fled, and the face of an adult woman began to replace it. "You saw—"

"I certainly hope none of the surviving Apple Valley fighters saw! How could you betray me like that?"

85

"Betray you?" She glared at him. "I kept an enemy sword from stabbing you in the back! I wouldn't let those men overpower you. Do you value your own life so little—"

"Come on, girl, I know what you're really upset about. Don't pretend."

"No, Uncle, this is not about what happened to Isaac." Several of the warriors eating around the room had stopped mid-bite and were watching the show. Rivka had always been headstrong, but never had she displayed such deadly calm and resolve in her outbursts. "He died because you imprisoned him, and yet I stayed to fight for you, to defend this keep, because this has been my home and I am part of this family, whether you like it or not. He died because of you and yet *I defended you*. And for that, you reject me?" The baron moved his mouth as if he wanted to interject, but she kept talking, her words fueled by the stinging nettles in her heart. "I reject *you*, Uncle. Thank you for my childhood. You don't deserve my talents. And you certainly do not deserve my respect. I. Am. Done. Here. Go shit in the sea."

Mitzi dashed out at her from a corner, a look of desperate pain across her face. "Rivka!"

"Mammeh, I'll send word. I love you, and some day if I settle down to guard one keep — which is what I've *always wanted*"— she glared at the baron — "I will send for you. And you'll still have a warm bed and good food, without his disdain."

There was one moment, during which nobody in the room — Rivka, Mitzi, the baron, the soldiers, the servants — moved at all. Then, with a final nod at her mother, Rivka turned around and stalked out, her sword at her side.

She lifted herself onto the huge mare and rode away. To her surprise, the mare reared suddenly and sprang up into the sky. The next thing she knew, she was riding a Dragon...

Chapter 11: Lighting the Candles

Rivka hadn't spoken much since trailing off at the end of her story, and the final hour of the ride was mostly silent. Shulamit felt an awkwardness that was practically tangible; it was likely Rivka was withdrawing after spending most of the day speaking about her past. She remembered her own parallel incidents — for example, those moments when she first told her ladies-in-waiting of her attraction toward other women — when she was shy after revealing her heart and found it clumsy to return to ordinary discourse. So she tried not to take it personally.

But it made for a tense afternoon. She was awed at the painful events she had heard, but had little of value to say in response. Fortunately, at least the weather and the dragon's stamina were both cooperating, and they arrived at a safe place to sleep without too much physical hardship.

"It's still light," said Rivka abruptly as she bustled around the rocks setting up their makeshift camp. "We should work on some of those self-defense techniques — if you're not fatigued from traveling." She didn't meet the queen's eyes.

"No, I'm ready. Like this?" Shulamit took a stance on the rock as Rivka had shown her.

She tried her best to concentrate on the movements, and managed about a half an hour of work before she realized she had pushed herself beyond where her muscles wanted to go. "Rivka, I'm sorry. I need to stop and eat."

"I'll send Dragon to go hunt us some food," said Rivka. "I saw some wild goats beyond the lake. That should give both of us more strength."

"How will she know not to catch birds first? Aviva taught me that even cooking my meat in the same pan as fowl can contaminate my food and cause... problems... and I see ducks in the water, in the reeds."

Rivka sighed, biting her lip. "I suppose I could ride with her and keep her to the goats. Do you feel safe waiting here for a few minutes by yourself?"

Shulamit weighed her options. After all she had been through, she still feared the assaults of unknown strangers. But she also had vivid, horrifying, humiliating memories of what would happen to her body if she ate anything tainted by the duck meat. Since it was something she'd experienced again and again, it rose up and took precedence. "I'll wait here. I think I see mint growing by the lake; I'll go collect some to season the goat."

"Good idea. I noticed wild tangerines growing over that way too." Rivka pointed.

Shulamit's face brightened at the idea of unexpected fresh fruit. She hurried off toward the lake as Rivka hopped onboard her dragon's back and leapt into the air.

Kneeling beside the lake gathering the choicest leaves from the wild mint plants into her lilac scarf brought back memories... scenes stored away close to her heart, wrapped in silk and scented with rose water.

❀ • ❀ • ❀

With each new food Aviva's experiments had cleared for Shulamit's safe consumption, the princess grew stronger and healthier. No more was she racked by daily digestive calamities; she had the energy to frolic in the palace gardens and enjoy life again. During the process, the two girls had become constant companions, and as Shulamit perked up, Aviva began teaching

89

her more about food preparation so that she could take charge of her own health more easily.

Aviva took her to the palace herb garden to teach her what all the herbs looked like. She plucked a handful of rippled green leaves and crushed them beneath Shulamit's nose. The cold, fresh scent flowed forth. "Is it singing to you?"

"It's mint!"

Aviva smiled in affirmation. "She smells cool because she keeps a secret part of herself always hidden away from the sun. She's strong enough to remain cold even in the hottest weather. She has principles and she sticks to 'em."

Shulamit giggled. "You always talk in poetry. Do you ever write anything down?"

A warm but slightly self-conscious smile spread over the cook's face. "I never thought of it as poetry — it just happens on its own when I talk. I get in a hurry to say what I'm feeling, and before I know it, I've said something goofy."

"I'm never bored around you," Shulamit observed. "Aviva—" Shulamit suddenly turned to face her and took one of her hands in both her own. She felt strength beneath the softness and warmth. "Why did you believe me? About being sick, I mean. When everyone else thinks it was in my head, or a ruse to look... well... princessy?"

"My mother's been sickly most of my life, so I know about illness and helping those who are ailing," Aviva explained. "When I was younger, I tended to her while my father moved mountains and reversed rivers all by himself. But now that I'm old enough I left home to go work, so I could replace the money she earned when she was a washerwoman. Aba's a tailor, and even though he'd rather be out in the marketplace selling his creations or visiting clients, if he stays home to take care of Ima, he can still take in mending and receive customers there. It's better for us all this

90

way. Maybe someday we'll even be able to afford surgery so she can walk again."

It awed Shulamit that this young woman, not two years older than herself, was financially contributing to her family in such a significant way. Especially since she, as the crown princess, was living a completely antithetical life. She felt undeserving and grateful that someone as incredible as Aviva even wanted to talk to her.

❀ • ❀ • ❀

Shulamit crushed the mint in her fingers, thinking about the relieving coolness who refused to compromise her ideas even in the face of something as powerful as the sun. She inhaled, and saw Aviva's dark, smiling face, her friendly eyes, the luscious curves of her body radiating femininity from beneath her sleeveless tunic and loose-fitting trousers. She could even hear that quirky, peasant-accented voice spouting its outlandish poetry.

With a sigh, she quickly gathered up the rest of the mint they needed and brought it back to the campsite. Rivka had left a pouch for her to use to collect tangerines both for tonight and for the rest of their journey, so she brought that back with her as she walked along the lakeshore to the wild grove.

But her heart wasn't finished replaying Aviva-infused memories. Her eyes were looking at fruit, picking the ones that were the most colorful and unblemished, but what she was in truth seeing was a scene from many months ago, when she had stolen away to Aviva's kitchen late at night.

❀ • ❀ • ❀

So much of that day was taken up by tutors, in their attempt to make up for time lost to digestive illness, that she had her fill neither of food nor of Aviva's company. It was several hours past moonrise by the time she finally tripped lightly down the path to the small building where all her meals were now prepared. It was a fowl-free, wheat-free, and most importantly, judgment- and doubt-free little paradise where all the food was edible and Shulamit was always believed.

It was far later than she had ever appeared there, so she knew Aviva wouldn't be expecting her. But what she herself wasn't expecting was the sight that greeted her eyes when she slipped unnoticed through the doorway.

Aviva was busily preparing a meal, most likely a trial run of some new experiment for Shulamit. But she didn't do so silently, and she wasn't merely cooking.

Instead, she was singing at the top of her lungs, a vivacious working-class dance tune. She was also using the handles of her knives, spoons, and other implements as drumsticks, beating them against the stone tables in time with her song. She twirled around the room, all hips and elbows, as she grabbed ingredients, chopped them up, and even tossed them into the dish in time to her dancing. She didn't know all the words, either — sometimes she just sang nonsense syllables.

Finally, she noticed the princess standing there watching her. She stopped dancing, put her hands on her hips, and said, "So what?"

Shulamit just giggled.

"Okay, so you see I've hidden a whole plague of frogs in my kitchen. Sometimes they do the work for me while they chirp." She paused to scoop up a handful of chopped herbs and toss it into the pot. "Well?"

92

"Well, what?"

"Now you know something embarrassing about me. So you should tell me something embarrassing about yourself. That way we're even."

"I like women the way men do," Shulamit blurted out, before she knew what she was doing. Heat crept into her face.

Aviva studied her from across the room for a moment, her head cocked like a bird's. Then she opened her mouth and began to sing again, and her feet began once again their dance. Only, this time, she held both of her hands out to Shulamit.

She didn't say anything about what Shulamit had admitted, but as she drew the princess close into their dance, it was clear that she was anything but scared away.

A cast-iron pot boiled over and interrupted their first kiss. Aviva rushed over to attend to it while Shulamit stood still, memorizing every detail — Aviva's soft mouth that tasted of fennel seeds, her full bosom pressed against Shulamit's own, those hands that made her feel so safe and well cared for. "Does the food agree with you?" asked Aviva, looking up from the stove with a wink.

Shulamit squeaked and then decided to nod instead of speaking. Embracing Aviva was like holding a huge bouquet of flowers in your arms, soft and glorious, with the scent overtaking you and pollen leaving yellow speckles across your nose.

"In my kitchen, there's always more for you to sample..."

❀ • ❀ • ❀

And then another, from months later:

Shulamit darted through the palace, slipping as silently as she could between rooms and courtyards. With nervous eyes she checked her path to make sure nobody was paying attention to her as she made her way toward Aviva's kitchen house for their prearranged tryst. Her jaws worked away at the fennel seeds she was chewing to make sure she wouldn't be repaying top-notch kisses with stale breath. Aviva kept saying she didn't care too much about Shulamit's ornaments, but the little princess didn't care and had bedecked herself in the clothing she thought prettiest: delicate fabrics of pastel-pink and lilac.

She rounded a corner, and her heart leapt; Aviva was rushing to meet her. The two women met in the corridor and joined hands. "We can't go back to my kitchen," Aviva explained. "The head chef is in there hiding from her flock — she was like a bag of tigers this morning and now she's too embarrassed to go back in there."

"But what's she doing?"

"Baking," said Aviva. "I know — I'll have to clean it all out again. I promise I'll be thorough."

"I wish there was a way to convince her I'm not just being picky!" Shulamit huffed. "Maybe I can help you clean when she finally leaves."

"It'll be like cleaning up for Passover."

Noises at both ends of the corridor made Shulamit tense up and whip her head in both directions, flinging her braids over her shoulders. "Someone's coming!"

"Quick! Come on!" Aviva grabbed her hand. There was a small door in the wall, leading into a cupboard, and Aviva pulled it open. Inside was a haphazard collection of rolled-up rugs, to be used in some of the palace hallways when the other rugs were dirty or a different color was required. The two girls could just fit *inside if they folded their limbs, and Aviva pulled the door shut just as several courtiers entered the hallway.*

They sounded as though they were arguing, but the door was thick and Shulamit couldn't make out any words. She was too busy kissing Aviva, and moving as best she could in the cramped space to get her arms around her. It was easy to be overwhelmed by the sensation of Aviva's lush body against her own, with her fleshy upper arms, large bosom, and generous hips.

Soon they were touching each other more intimately, and Shulamit moaned into the tender place on Aviva's neck where she rested her head. Her left hand was full of one of Aviva's breasts, the feel of which sent her brain spiraling into pinwheels of delight. "I tried looking in books to see why these make me so happy," she commented. "Nobody knew."

Aviva giggled at her. "You would." Moans overtook her ability to speak as she ground herself harder against Shulamit's other hand.

"It wasn't a complete waste of time — I did find some pretty interesting reading on how our bodies work."

Aviva clenched her teeth, clearly trying to muffle herself, but the next groan escaped anyway, even stronger. "Is that why you're — Ahhh! Okay, you studied for sex. You are truly amazing."

"The book said if I—" Shulamit altered the movement of her fingers slightly.

Aviva let out a noise like wind rustling through palm fronds before a storm. "Smart book. Good book. Gonna make... halvah... for the... book...ohh..."

Then Shulamit felt like a magician, the same way she did every time she'd achieved the seemingly miraculous feat of making Aviva climax. She made sure to continue what she'd been doing until Aviva calmed down, and then concentrated on the sensations of her own body until she followed her.

"We're gonna have such backaches after being in here," she commented, snuggling into Aviva's warmth.

"We still have to work it off cleaning out my kitchen after we've got it back to ourselves!"

"Mmmm." Shulamit inhaled deeply. The inside of the little cupboard smelled of woman, and she felt dizzyingly content.

❀ • ❀ • ❀

Shulamit was so lost in the heat of these passionate memories that she gathered far more tangerines than she had intended. Not wanting to waste them, she carried them all back to the campsite and began juicing them into one of the drinking vessels.

It was getting darker, and the sun had started to paint the sky brilliant colors with its departure, so she was relieved to see her companion returning. Dragon clutched a slain goat in the claws of her back legs like an eagle holding a rabbit. "This will feed us for several days," said Rivka. She was acting like herself again.

"What about Dragon? Or — wait, she feeds as a horse. I'm confused."

"I let her feed first."

"That makes sense. I picked too many tangerines, so I've been juicing them. And here's the mint."

Rivka butchered the goat and set it up over the fire to cook. Then she stood up and gazed out over the lake at the sunset.

"It's Shabbat," Shulamit suddenly realized out loud.

Rivka muttered quietly in her own language in a cadence Shulamit took for counting out the days. "So it is. There's our Shabbas candle..."

"Where?" Shulamit felt smart for noticing Rivka's usage of the northern version of the word.

Rivka pointed at the sunset, a pink-and-gold marvel that spread across the far shore of the lake. "And the lake can be the wine."

"We can say the wine blessing over the tangerine juice," Shulamit suggested.

Rivka grinned. "That's the idea." Then a look of horror spread across her face. "You can't eat challah!"

"I know. I miss it."

"Never mind, I don't know why I said that." Rivka shook her head at her own bluntness.

Shulamit shrugged. "I miss sufganiyot more, especially at Chanukah when everyone has them at once. But Aviva used to fry me sweet plantains instead. I like the bits that get a little burnt the best."

"What are sufganiyot?"

"Fried dough with sugar on top."

"We fry potato pancakes for Chanukah."

"That sounds good. I can eat potato," said Shulamit. "We'd better start before the colors start fading. They're so... they go away so quickly. Sometimes the prettiest part only lasts a minute."

The two women sat down and covered their eyes to say a blessing, and then looked out over the beautiful sunset.

As they waited for the goat to cook, their talk turned to business. "What do you think it's going to be like when we get to the sorcerer's keep?" Shulamit asked.

"From what Tamar told me, it sounded like he's actually a pretty big coward," said Rivka, peeling a tangerine with her thumbs. "All the sleazy behavior toward women — he tends to keep that in check when men are around. He was singing to one of them, once, and stopped right in the middle and refused to continue because a man showed up to deliver rice. And did you hear what she said about how paranoid he was? He even told some of the holy women bad things about himself so that he could 'expose' the truth as a lie — preemptively, since it turned out that nobody had warned anyone at all."

"I remember her saying that," said Shulamit. "I bet someone cowardly, paranoid, and skilled in magic would protect himself with plenty of enchantments."

Rivka nodded. "Exactly. So you've been thinking about it too."

Shulamit nodded. "It's keeping my mind off Aviva. The smell of the mint brought back... things."

"I'm sorry about that," said Rivka. "But thinking is good. I like the way your mind works. Back there in the inn, you really impressed me with the way you solved that crime."

Shulamit smiled and pulled her knees up to her chest, hugging them. "That felt amazing," she admitted, "once I knew I wasn't going to die, of course!"

"Nobody said you can't be a queen and solve crimes at the same time," Rivka pointed out. "Wisdom and justice are traits that will earn the respect and trust of your people."

"I wanted to solve a mystery back home once," said Shulamit. "Money was stolen from my father's treasury. Only a few people had keys, but he trusted them all. He wouldn't let me ask questions, and he never did find out what happened."

Rivka studied her with darkened eyes. "Does that have anything to do with the elephant?"

Shulamit shook her head quickly. "No, that was just a freak accident. He was pushing himself too hard — not enough sleep — working all day and then trying to spend time with me *and* his lady friends *and* hobbies, athletics... he was trying to do everything." She sighed heavily. "Maybe he got all his living done fast, and if he'd have lived slower, he'd have lived longer."

"Maybe," said Rivka. "Or maybe a *howdah* is just a terrible place for an exhausted man of any age."

"I feel safer on Dragon than up on an elephant now."

"She's a good girl." Rivka smiled and patted the beast. "Oh, hey, the goat's ready."

They fed themselves as quickly as the hot meat would allow them. "Can we go back to practicing after dinner?" Rivka asked.

"On Shabbat?"

Rivka just raised one eyebrow.

"I guess you're right."

"Tomorrow afternoon we face our enemy," Rivka reminded her. "I don't want you should get killed."

"I'll concentrate twice as hard," Shulamit announced proudly.

Chapter 12: The Honey Trap

The next morning, they set out for the sorcerer's mountain stronghold. Dragon's flight took them over areas of rocky ground and deep chasms that no horse and definitely no pair of humans could have made on foot, and Shulamit was nervously thankful that she had enough energy to get off the ground.

Finally, in the afternoon, they reached the keep. A proud, high sun illuminated a tower of stone carved straight into the mountainside. Leading up to the tower was a gravel walkway edged with larger stones and planted with olive trees. Dragon landed at the edge of the walkway and morphed into her horse form. After Rivka and Shulamit dismounted, she swept her sensitive muzzle over the rocks, devouring any blade of grass she could find.

"She's tiring," Rivka observed. Then she turned to Shulamit. "You should remove that."

"What?"

Rivka fingered the lilac scarf around Shulamit's neck. "Very pretty, but look." She grabbed the scarf and jerked it suddenly.

Shulamit froze up in panic and nearly burst into tears even though it was only a mock attack. After producing an embarrassing gasping noise, she nodded, eyeing Rivka as if she were not entirely certain her demonstration had been in good taste.

"Hey, I'm sorry." Rivka offered her arm. "*Nu*, did I make my point?"

Shulamit fell into the comforting hug and then quickly put the scarf away in her bag.

Rivka swept her fingers over her sword hilt. "Well? Let's go see what there is to see." She led her queen and her steed down the gravel path.

Pebbles crunched beneath their feet. "He really likes stone, doesn't he?" Shulamit observed. "He lives in stone, with little stones leading up to it, and he turned the holy women into stone." She paused for a moment, working on an idea.

Rivka took another step.

The larger stones at the side of the path began to spit spherical golden blobs at them. "What?!" Shulamit shrieked.

Rivka tried to dodge the assault, but it was coming from so many directions that it was impossible. Before long, both women and even the horse were covered in—

"*Honey?*" Rivka lifted her eyebrow. "I don't underst—"

Then the stones firing honey balls rotated ninety degrees and switched ammunition. Tiny, hard particles spewed out at the travelers from all angles. Rivka batted at the storm with both hands, trying to protect her face. "I'm glad I took off my scarf!" Shulamit wailed, looking down at her clothing.

"*These* are his enchantments to keep out invaders?" bellowed Rivka. "What is this, *grain*? Shula, make sure it doesn't get in your mou—"

"Your eyes! Cover your eyes!" Shulamit suddenly screamed.

"*Nu?*" And then Rivka stopped asking questions, because a flock of crazed birds was descending all around them. Drawn by the seeds spat out by their master's magical rocks, the cloud of brightly colored flapping hellions closed in on the warrior and the queen. Shulamit shrank to the ground and pulled her body into as tiny a ball as she could manage, whereas Rivka unsheathed her sword with one hand while covering her eyes with the elbow of the other.

101

Then they heard a familiar, welcome sound — the much louder, deeper flap of the dragon's wings. It only took a few mighty blows for her to drive away the birds. Rivka uncovered her eyes and watched Dragon dispatch the last few birds, scaring away the quick and munching on the slower. "Good girl," she said with a relieved smile, and patted the beast's scaly avocado-rind hide. "You deserve that little nosh. I hope it's tasty."

Shulamit was still sitting on the ground, trying to clean herself off. "I'm disgusting. Wait, did the two things I can't eat just *attack* me?"

"Just be careful, so it won't get in your mouth." Then Rivka let out an uncharacteristic giggle, because Dragon had transformed back into a horse and was licking some of the foul honey-birdseed mixture off her face. "*Oy.* Don't even talk to me about disgusting."

"I see water up there." Shulamit sprang up and made a beeline for the large stone fountain near the entrance of the fortress.

Rivka and the horse followed her. "If it's even water," Rivka muttered, "and not borscht, at this rate."

The horse sneezed. "You're right," Rivka added, as if the horse's sneeze had meant something. "We're too far south for borscht."

Shulamit reached the fountain but then hesitated. "Riv! What if it's *not* water?"

"I was joking."

"I know, but — he's a sorcerer. What if it's poison or acid or something?"

Rivka lifted one eyebrow. "Good thinking. Only one way to find out!" She plunged one hand into the water. "Seems safe to me."

Shulamit's mouth dropped open. Sometimes Rivka's bravery scared her. She smiled, but it was a horrified smile.

"I should taste it just to double-check," Rivka mused. But the horse had ambled up beside her and was drinking out of the fountain herself with no ill effects.

The two women began to scrub off the honey and birdseed. As they washed, a young woman ran out of the fortress. She was exceedingly lovely, and her hands were bound. Her feet had been bound too, but the rope was cut roughly, as if against a stone. Barely a wisp of clothing hid a dark, luxurious landscape of a body. Her hair had been pinned up behind each ear but the pins were coming down as if she hadn't been able to tend to it in a while. "At last! Finally, someone will rescue me!"

Rivka quickly secured her cloth face-mask and turned to face her. "Rescue you? You're a prisoner here?"

The woman nodded. "Yes. I'm Ori. The bird-master took me from my people and tried to make me his wife. Again and again, I refused, but he won't let me go. I heard movement on the path and managed to cut some of my bindings, in hopes that you would take me away with you. I can't leave this place by myself — not on foot. The surrounding lands are too rocky, and I couldn't run away. But now that you've come, I'll be saved!" She exhaled happily, her bosom rising and falling and her hardened nipples visible through the sheer fabric of her dress.

Shulamit was entranced. Moving closer, she undid the rope around Ori's wrists and then took one hand in both of hers. "Of course we'll save you." The beautiful captive smelled of flowers, and her hand was soft and warm. Shulamit suddenly wanted to kiss her very badly, and she was astonished to see Ori gazing at her as if she were thinking the same thing.

Rivka stayed back, studying the scene critically. "We can't leave right away — we're here for a purpose. We have... business with the sorcerer."

"I'll show you the way into the keep. Come! Quickly!" Ori ran toward the door.

Shulamit made as if to follow, but Rivka caught her by one hand. The queen turned around in confusion, but Rivka gave her a hard look. "Don't follow her."

"What? Why not? Rivka, she could be the one! Maybe the reason God got me mixed up in this rescue mission instead of just sending you by yourself was because she's the woman I'm out here looking for."

"Put your tongue back in your head, Queenling. She's no good."

"What are you talking about? She's just another one of his victims."

"I don't think so. She feels wrong." Rivka was speaking very quietly so Ori couldn't hear.

"Come, warriors!" called Ori from the doorway.

Rivka picked up one of the pebbles from the path and chucked it through the door. It was a good three seconds before they heard a tiny *tock* noise — a noise that clearly came from much farther away.

"See? No floor." Rivka was still holding Shulamit's wrist and dragged the queen behind her as she stalked around the fortress entrance. "That's not the real way in."

"But what about Ori?"

"She's there to lure intruders to fall to their deaths," Rivka explained. "See, she has no effect on me — I bet it never occurred to that *schmendrick* that women would ever try to break in. He just thinks of women as prizes, not people."

"She wouldn't catch a man if he were like me, either," observed the queen with a somber face. "But he probably isn't too worried about them."

"I wouldn't be surprised if she were just an illusion," Rivka added. "She's not coming after us. Follow me this way while I look for a real entrance."

Both human and horse obeyed. Shulamit glanced back down the rocky path at Ori, who was still looking after them with big sad eyes — but, as Rivka said, without any attempt to call them back. She felt foolish.

But she quickly redeemed herself. "Hey! There!"

Rivka studied the spot where Shulamit was pointing. It appeared to be just more solid rock face, with the type of texture that happens when a slice of rock sheers off and falls to the ground — but its solidness was an illusion. Part of the rock was actually *behind* the section of rock beside it, and it was possible to slip between the two and venture inside. "Good work, Queenling!"

Shulamit smiled with half her face.

The women and the horse stepped inside and found themselves in a dark hall of stone, lit only by skylights. There was nowhere to walk except forward, so they proceeded down the hallway. Their footsteps echoed in the cold, dark-gray world. It was cooler in here than outside, and silent, and felt terrifyingly timeless. By the time they reached the door at the end of the passageway, several minutes had gone by and they could no longer even see any light from the entrance through which they had come — only the feeble light from above.

Rivka put a firm grip on the door handle and pulled it forward.

The next room was better lit, and decorated with all manner of military artifacts. "Wow," Rivka exclaimed breathily. "These aren't just from Perach — those over there are from Imbrio, and Zembluss, and some of the other little countries to the north. I remember meeting them in battle."

"There are so many different types." Shulamit peered around at the abundance and disarray.

"Look over there." Rivka pointed to the far side of the room, a wistful note in her voice. "Those armor and weapons are from my homeland. And *those* — I've never even seen those in person. I just recognize them from Isaac's history books." She paused. "I bet he could identify every single thing in this room. *Oy vey iz mir*, Queenling, do I miss him..."

Shulamit didn't say anything, because she couldn't find the right words to comfort her. But into the silence there suddenly came a horrible noise, a rough clang like metal falling into metal. Then two of the suits of armor began to pace forward from the wall, toward the women. Rivka stepped out in front of Shulamit and unsheathed her sword. She held it at the ready, eyes narrowed.

Chapter 13: The Sorcerer's Arsenal

Both soulless suits of armor picked up a sword and brandished it. Shulamit's eyes went from one to the other. They looked identical. Rivka stood at the ready, head held high, clearly waiting for one of them to do something.

"You protect a worthless child!" rasped the one on the right, glaring at Rivka. "A spoiled princess is no queen."

Shulamit, cowering behind Rivka, gritted her teeth. "Don't listen to them!" hissed Rivka. "I don't know what they're up to."

"What right have you to seek a woman for your sweetheart, when those women who work hard for their living may never be able to follow their true nature?" continued the disembodied male voice from the armor on the right. "You are an undeserving fool."

"I'm not a fool!" Shulamit shouted. "I may be pampered, but at least my brain works. A brain that you don't even *have*, you overgrown tin drinking vessel!" But her face was hot, and her heart was pounding.

Then the armor on the left lifted his sword against Rivka. She blocked the blow and began to fight him, leaving Shulamit unprotected from the other suit of armor. It stomped around the fighting pair to face Shulamit. "No sword? Do you expect to escape me with the pathetic bits of self-defense this harpy has been teaching you?"

"No, not really!" Shulamit darted across the room and climbed into a small alcove behind a display cabinet full of daggers. The suit of armor followed, swinging its sword. She was trapped, but at least she was so far inside her hiding place that its reach was too short to injure her.

"What right have you to jeopardize your father's kingdom by not marrying to produce an heir? Perach should never have been trusted to a freak like you."

Shulamit narrowed her eyes and gritted her teeth. "I don't have to think about that yet." But she knew it was right, at least about the heir.

"You think you're so smart, but look how distracted you were when Ori's nipples were pointing at you outside! You could be so easily manipulated." The suit of armor crashed its sword against the display cabinet, shattering its glass.

Shulamit pulled herself tighter into a ball and shut her eyes to protect herself from the flying shards. She was still ashamed about Ori. Wasn't this whole trip unfair to the kingdom in some way? If she died here, in this castle, because she'd gone off looking for feminine companionship, it would just prove she'd been too broken to rule from the start. She'd worried about that from the beginning, especially because liking women wasn't the only surprise her body had thrown at her.

"One day, your subjects will see you sick from your food, and, oh, will they be disgusted!" shouted the suit of armor. "How could anybody touch such a body with love, a body that spews filth without control?"

Shulamit covered her face at the images its words were putting into her head.

"Useless daughter of indolence!" it shouted at her. "It's no surprise your lover lost patience with you!"

Shulamit burst into tears.

"Of course she stayed for a while, your slutty cook, but she likes men too — you had to have known you wouldn't be able to keep her forever. Why would she stay with you when she could go off and have a real family with a husband to satisfy her properly?"

The suit of armor stomped on the floor angrily, then began trying to rip the display cabinet off the wall so it could get at Shulamit. One entire shelf of the cabinet broke off in its mighty grip, and this it tossed inside the alcove. She ducked and squished her body farther against the corner.

This was it. Rivka was busy fighting the other suit of armor and couldn't rescue her, and she was going to die. Desperately, she whimpered, "Aba..." hoping that he would at least come down and get her and make it not hurt so much.

Then she noticed that the suit of armor was having trouble ripping up the cabinet. It couldn't muster the strength to tear off another shelf the way it had the first one. "Heartless walking fork," said Shulamit bitterly, wiping away a tear that was dripping off her nose. "If you feed on negative thoughts, why don't you just go for the mother lode? I lost my father. That should make you strong enough to knock down the wall — the whole castle!"

The suit of armor stumbled in confusion. Shulamit was confused too. The more overwhelmed by filial grief she felt, the less effective against her were its attacks. "Okay," she mumbled to herself. "It's not feeding on negative emotion. It's feeding on insecurity. Well, then, *I am completely amazing.*" She walked out of the alcove, head held high, her arms folded across her chest. "I'm smart. I may not have grown up working hard, but I'm not afraid to do it when I have to. Maybe Aviva did run away because she got tired of me, but *I like myself.* And I swear on my father's grave *I will never let my people down just because I'm different.*"

The suit of armor was standing completely motionless, but it still held its gleaming sword. Trembling, Shulamit reached out and took the weapon away from it.

She had no idea what to do with it once she had it, but now the suit was unarmed, and that was the important thing.

She scurried back to Rivka and was shocked to discover that the warrior maiden wasn't doing so well. There was nothing flawed in her swordplay, but the suit of armor was stronger than she was, and had a skill beyond any that she had ever encountered.

Shulamit listened to what it was saying. "—act without thinking, leading to *death*! You've always known that had you been more careful, Isaac would never have died," rasped the armor in a flat, unemotional drone. "On long, lonely nights you've thought about how you should have gone straight up to his room once you discovered your sword was no longer secret. If you had gone to his room instead *and taken his sword*, you would have been armed when confronting your uncle. Those men couldn't have held you, and he would have had no sway over Isaac. Together, the two of you could have fought your way out of the room and run away together. What have you cheated yourself out of, Rivka bat Beet-Greens? Think of the years together you've lost. Think of his voice, his eyes—"

"Don't listen to it, Rivka! It feeds on insecurity," Shulamit shrieked.

"I don't care!" Rivka screamed back in agony. "It's right!" She kept on fighting, but her breath heaved with fatigue.

"Instead, you jumped in—" the armor continued.

"I acted quickly out of bravery," Rivka insisted.

"Every brave act you have ever committed is tainted with what loss that bravery has wrought! Every time you rode, fearless, into battle, was disgraced by how your impetuousness cost you your wizard."

Shulamit, heady at her own victory over the armor, thought quickly. "No, Rivka! Remember? Remember how, as soon as your uncle had the sword, he sent the four guards to capture you? You didn't even know they'd found the sword. Four guards showed up at your room, and burst in—"

"What are you—?"

Shulamit watched a change come over Rivka's face and hoped she was beginning to understand — she needed to picture the events as Shulamit described them, not as they were. "Remember how horrible it felt to have Lev's hands on your body? Remember his terrible breath? Remember the feel of the daggers poking against your skin?" The memories were from the Great Hall, when the baron had commanded his guards to clap hold of her, but Rivka had to imagine them taking place in her room instead — or else they were lost.

"You had no choice, no opportunity to make a decision," Shulamit continued.

Rivka concentrated on the lie. Soon, the suit of armor was more manageable, and eventually, she defeated it. Kicking it over with a loud yell, she grabbed its sword and tossed it into a corner. "Come on! The door!"

They ran toward the door on the other side of the room, the horse following soon after. As soon as they were through, they banged it shut and leaned back against it.

Rivka turned to look at Shulamit. "None of that was true."

"No, but I needed to save our lives," Shulamit pointed out.

"Thank you," said Rivka. She was silent for a moment. "I can't run away from that, though. I was impulsive and stupid and didn't think, and now Isaac is gone. If I could do it over..."

Shulamit didn't know what to say, so she looked around the new room instead. "Is that a crystal ball?"

The new room was full of dusty books and lit by sunlight pouring in through several open windows, but the table in the center of the room held a crystal ball. "It looks like it," said Rivka. She approached the table. "Maybe I should ask it where the antidote is. Then we won't even have to fight the sorcerer." She held out her hand—

Then the horse suddenly broke into a gallop, indoors though they were, and kicked the entire table over so hard the crystal ball was shot clear through one of the windows. Rivka and Shulamit ran to the window, but it was too late to catch it. One of the birdmaster's birds was flying past the window, and the unfortunate creature was right in the trajectory. Upon touching it, the ball exploded into an orange fireball. The smoke rushed toward the women, and they quickly drew back from the window, coughing and rubbing their pained eyes.

"That could have been me," Rivka said in shock. She put her arms around Dragon's neck and rested her head against her mane for a moment.

"How on earth—?" Shulamit looked at the horse, then at the table. Then she followed Rivka into the next room.

Except for the intruders, this room was empty. It was a plain but somehow proportionally pleasant room, with plenty of sunlight and pretty much nothing else. "I don't get it," said Rivka, crankily. "What's going to explode this time?"

Shulamit pondered. "The bird attack was supposed to get rid of, well, most people trying to get in. Then there was Ori, the suits of armor, and the exploding ball. So, anyone who made it in here isn't that interested in women, doesn't have strong insecurities, and has no inclination to look into the future. I'm getting an image in my mind of a very holy man — someone completely enlightened. You know what? I bet the idea is that an enlightened man would enter this room and then never leave. This room's too perfect. He'd just sit here forever, pondering the universe."

"Too enlightened to have a sex drive, insecurities, or curiosity," grumbled Rivka. "The two of us, that's not! *Oy gevalt.*"

"Yes, but if we had brought Sister Tamar along with us, we'd be carrying her away over our shoulders." Shulamit grinned mischievously.

"How *do* we get out of here?" Rivka wondered aloud, peering around. "The only way out, besides the windows, seems to be..."

"Up there?"

The ceiling of the room rose far higher on the far side than where they stood, and if they squinted they could make out a second level to the room, almost approximating a loft. "*Nu*, Dragon?"

The horse walked up to them and transformed, but when they climbed onto her back, her wings flapped uselessly without lifting anyone into the air. "What's the matter?"

"She needs rest," Rivka pointed out.

They sat there on her back for a few more minutes until she was finally able to push, push, *push* herself upward. With a few last flaps of her wings, she landed safely on the loft and then abruptly curled up, breathing heavily. Her wings drooped uselessly at her sides like wilted beet greens.

From atop the dragon's back, the women surveyed the scene before them. This had apparently been one of the sorcerer's living quarters, but it was in utter disarray. All across the room lay upturned and broken furniture, and smaller objects like books and goblets were scattered here and there at random.

And there, in the center of the chamber before them on a large rug of intricate geometric design, existed two unexpected sights.

One of them was a man of indeterminate age, dark-skinned like Shulamit's people but with hair in a foreign style, and wearing dark-blue robes, sprawled out on the rug. His face was contorted in agony, and the open-eyed stare over his jowly cheeks proclaimed him dead as dumplings. In his fist he clutched a crystal vial with a gold rim; only a few drops of the blue liquid inside remained in the very bottom corners.

The other sight was a voluptuous young woman, collapsed on the rug with her eyes closed, her clothing torn open and her limbs sticking out at odd angles. It was Aviva, and she wasn't moving.

Chapter 14: Bittersweet Discoveries

Shulamit scrambled down off the dragon's back so fast she lost her bearing. She landed hard on one unprepared arm and yowled in pain as her wrist protested the abuse. Rivka deftly dismounted and rushed to her side.

"I'm okay. I'm okay." Shulamit gasped, holding her arm close to her body. "Rivka, that's Aviva." No more words could she utter in her stunned amazement.

She tried to move toward the fallen girl, but Rivka intercepted her. "Can you move it?"

Shulamit experimented, and yelped at the result. "Ow-oww!"

Rivka felt up and down the afflicted limb. "I think you just sprained it. Just... take it easy for now. Or — wait. Where's that silk scarf?"

"Here." Shulamit took it out of her bag with her good hand, and Rivka quickly wrapped it around the sprain.

As soon as she was free of Rivka's protective grasp, she dashed to Aviva's side, ignoring the gnawing, twisted pain in her own arm. She put her good hand to Aviva's shoulder and drew back in horror when she felt something cold and hard instead of the warm, pliant flesh she was expecting. Not dead! — But, no, not dead, for now that she was close enough she could hear that Aviva still breathed.

Timidly but steadily, she brought her hand to Aviva's cheek and touched two fingers to her temple. The skin of her face was warm and human. Shulamit's fingers slid down the side of her cheek down to her jawline.

A weak sound came from the other girl's throat, from behind closed lips. Then, finally, her lips parted. "Wa..."

115

"She needs water," shouted Rivka, bounding over from across the room where she'd been studying the corpse of what was most likely the sorcerer. "Here." She thrust one of the drinking vessels at Shulamit, who held it to Aviva's mouth.

Tangerine juice dribbled out onto Aviva's parched lips. Shulamit held the vessel carefully, and then slid her injured arm around Aviva's head to cradle her face upward slightly. She forced herself to ignore the pain and just concentrate on making sure most of the juice went into Aviva's mouth instead of running down her chin.

Finally, Aviva's lips began to move, helping the juice along, and then her eyes slowly opened. When she tried to speak it was in an unintelligible mumble, but Shulamit caught the word 'dream.' "I'm not a dream," said the queen. "It's really me."

Aviva couldn't say anything more, but a radiant look lit her gaunt face.

"We need to get more into her. She looks like she hasn't eaten for days." Rivka, in her exploration of the room, had found a side entrance that led into a small galley-style kitchen. She was opening cabinet doors and peering inside jars, looking for anything suitable.

"Riv—" Shulamit studied the body of her runaway sweetheart with a growing sense of understanding. "I think — it's like the holy women. Part of her — *most* of her's been turned to stone, but her head and this bit of her neck are still awake." She lifted one of Aviva's hands from the rug, and it came up much more easily than she had anticipated. "And where she's stone, it's not heavy like real stone. It's as light as if she were hollow."

"I found broth. Here. She'll need it to get strong again." Rivka brought over a drinking vessel she had found in the kitchen, filled with a broth that, from the smell of it, had been made from lamb or goat. "It's not hot, but that's not important."

Shulamit kept feeding her the nourishing liquid. "If that's the sorcerer over there, and she's been mostly turned to stone, I bet he cursed her before he died, but then died before the curse was complete."

"That makes sense." Rivka kept looking all around the room. "I hope there's another bottle of that curse blight Tamar kept talking about. The one he's holding is nearly empty, and I don't know how we're going to turn that entire courtyard of women *plus* your stone girlfriend over there back into regular human beings, with barely a full drop left."

"There's got to be another one somewhere around here."

"Why?"

"Because... bah." Shulamit had nearly said something as inane as *Because I'm the queen.* She was frantic with worry over Aviva, and since she still didn't know why Aviva had left in the first place, she was also filled with anxiety about whether or not Aviva wanted anything to do with her once she had nursed her back to health.

She tried to reassure herself by thinking of the happy look in Aviva's eyes when she had recognized Shulamit and realized she was real, but hey, maybe she was just happy to be rescued. Right now that was more important, anyway. Even if she didn't want to talk to her after she was safe, there was no way Shulamit would ever just leave her there.

They remained there for quite some time — Shulamit feeding Aviva meat broth or tangerine juice or water from Rivka's canteen, then letting her rest; Rivka stalking about the room, poring over old books and peeping in every cubbyhole she could find; and Dragon resting in the corner of the room.

Then, weakly, from Aviva's mouth, came, "Thank you."

Sun rose on Shulamit's face. "Aviva! I—"

117

"I can't move," said Aviva.

"I think the sorcerer turned you to stone," said Shulamit. "I mean — that man over there — the dead one. Was he the sorcerer?"

"Yes, that was the bird man," said Aviva. "He's dead because he went hunting in the wrong forest, and the trees... rose up and swallowed him whole."

"I missed hearing you do that. But I still don't understand."

Aviva glanced down at her torn clothing, then back up at Shulamit — who had been trying to ignore the flesh exposed by the tears, especially since it was now disturbingly stone. "I came here as his hired cook and chambermaid. But he was an awful man, always looking for the next woman to pester. I knew that someday he'd try to force himself on me. So every morning after I bathed, I ground a fatal herb and spread it across my bosom. I knew that's where he'd start. Everyone seems to start there, with me... I guess it's only natural, with their size."

Shulamit flushed and wanted to cover her face with her hands because she fit neatly into that category herself, but she suppressed the impulse. "So, he ripped open your clothes, and...?"

"Got a mouthful of poison for his trouble," said Aviva. "He screamed at me that I was a witch, and drank the whole bottle of curse blight trying to save himself. But I'm not a witch, and herbs aren't magic. It wasn't a curse. It was just a poisonous plant. The curse blight did nothing. So he cursed me, but he had his final seizure and died before the curse finished. And then I must have fallen asleep because I couldn't move, and I've had nothing to eat or drink in days. Oh, Lord, I'm so weak!"

Shulamit quickly fed her more broth, then began peeling a tangerine for her. "Aviva, I'm a terrible person for not waiting to ask this, but I'm going to explode if I don't know. Why did you leave the palace? What did I do?"

Aviva closed her eyes, and her face contorted with painful memory. "It had nothing to do with you. Nathan said he'd pay for my mother to have surgery that would make her nearly well again if I left the palace and never spoke to you again. I'm so sorry! That's why I was such a cactus those last few days. I had to do it. She's my *mother*."

"Nathan? The captain of Aba's guard?"

Aviva nodded. "He thought I was too lowborn to be seen... amusing you." She looked as if she wanted to crawl into a hole.

"He's a fool. And where did he get the money to pay for that surgery, anyway? He has seven children!"

"I don't know anything about that," said Aviva. "I just know it was a bag of old coins with a picture of your great-grandfather on them."

Shulamit's mouth dropped open. For several seconds she was unable to speak. Then she squeaked out, "I can't believe it. Rivka! Hey, Riv!" For a moment, she had forgotten to keep Rivka's identity private, but then she recovered.

Rivka bounded over, the curse-blight bottle in her hand. "*Nu?*"

"Remember that money I was telling you about? The money stolen from my father's treasury? Apparently, the captain of the guard took it, and used it to — What insolence! What betrayal! Aviva—"

"I didn't know!" Aviva protested.

"Not *you*," Shulamit reassured her hastily. "You did what you had to."

"Well, I certainly reject my promise to him, now that I know the money wasn't his to give."

119

"*Good*, because I'm taking you back! I mean — will you — I know I—"

"Mint is cold and can resist the sun's heat by the strength of her convictions," said Aviva, "but mint is a plant, and plants wither and die without the sun." She looked up at Shulamit lovingly. "I hated it. I had to, but I hated it. I always wanted to stay with you."

"If Nathan were here right now, I'd fire him right on the spot! I want Riv to take his place anyway, but even though I'm queen, it's still hard to stand up to those guards sometimes! This will give me a good reason. Oh," she suddenly realized. "Aviva, this is Riv, the new captain of my royal guard."

"Hello," said Aviva. "I'm a cook, made of stone. Nice to meet you."

"Charmed," said Rivka, bowing.

"I'm sorry to call you Your Majesty," said Aviva, her face suddenly growing solemn.

"Then don't," urged Shulamit, taking one stone hand in hers, even though she knew Aviva probably couldn't feel it. "I'm always just your Shulamit."

"I'm grateful for that — that you can still say that after the way I left."

"You left because you were too good a person to let your mother go on in anguish and your father in a lifetime of service simply so you could be happy. How am I supposed to not love you *more* for being that kind of person?"

Aviva smiled briefly, and then her face grew cloudy again. "But, Shulamit, that's not what I meant. I'm sorry to call you Your Majesty instead of Your Highness."

Shulamit's face fell. "Oh."

"I cried for you. While all of Perach mourned our king, I mourned Shulamit's father. I'm so sorry."

"Maybe your mother and father would come to the palace to live with us," Shulamit suggested. "My parents are both gone. In fact, I have very few people in the world that I like right now. You, and Riv, and sometimes my ladies-in-waiting when they aren't being tiresome."

"I hope you'll like them," said Aviva, smiling at the idea.

Then Aviva wanted to know how Shulamit and Rivka had come to the fortress, so they told her about the holy women who had been turned to stone. "I don't know what we're going to do if we can't find another bottle of curse blight," said Rivka.

"That's the only one," Aviva affirmed sadly. "And if he'd had more, he would have drained them too. He shouldn't have touched me..."

Shulamit was thinking again. "Aviva, is the magic in that bottle very strong?"

"The strongest," said Aviva. "It hardly takes any."

"But how would we get it spread across eighteen or nineteen grown women? Not to mention you there?" Rivka put her hands on her hips and sighed.

"There's that basin of holy water on the roof," suggested the queen. "If the magic is powerful enough, we could put the bottle at the bottom of the basin, and then... if Sister Tamar lets us... we could knock down the front of the basin. The water would spill down into the courtyard, and—"

"—soak all the women at once. I think it could work!" said Rivka.

"Can you smash the basin?"

121

The warrior shrugged. "Probably. I don't know. I'll try. If it doesn't work, we'll have to carry it down the stairs in buckets one at a time."

"At least we have a place to start."

"Now that we have a plan, are we ready to get out of here?" Rivka put the crystal vial deep inside her clothing where it would be safe.

Dragon made a show of flapping her wings, to show that they weren't strong enough yet.

"Flying can't be the only way in or out of this room," said Rivka. "Unless these two have wings I don't see." She was pointing at the dead body and the mostly stone woman.

"Oh, there are stairs back down into the rest of the fortress," said Aviva. "They come out of the rock on his command. All the stones of this place obey him."

"That explains the rock walkway shooting honey and birdseed at us on the way in," said Shulamit.

"That doesn't do us any good. He can't command anymore." Rivka paced the room.

"It wasn't so much a command," Aviva explained, "as him putting his hand on the wall in the right place."

"He's still got hands," Shulamit remarked.

Rivka took a hold of the sorcerer's lifeless wrist and dragged him over to the wall. "Where?"

"Higher."

Rivka hoisted him up, while Shulamit marveled at her ability to play with a dead body without flinching. "Here?"

"Right where that crack is, between the two smaller rocks."

122

Rivka pressed the dead man's fist against the spot.

There was a low rumble. Far away, there was the sound of something crashing to the ground. Then the floor began to vibrate disconcertingly.

"That's not supposed to happen," said Aviva.

"The stone!" Shulamit cried with alarm. "It obeys his command, but now it can tell he's dead."

Rivka steadied herself as the room started to shake. "It didn't know before?"

"No, he died on the rug so his dead body hadn't touched the stone." Shulamit dragged Aviva out of the way of a falling piece of rocky ceiling. "All those enchantments and traps—"

Rivka's eyes flared in horror. "I bet he set this whole place to collapse if something happened to him!"

Chapter 15: Is It Here That I Learn Fear?

"Hurry, Shula! Dragon!" Rivka ran over to Aviva and hefted the poor girl over her shoulder, then followed the queen to the beast. With the three of them on her back, the dragon scrabbled around the room on foot, trying her best to dodge falling rocks. Her wings flapped at her sides, trying to gain elevation.

"It's not working!" Shulamit burst into tears.

"Why is your dragon broken?" Aviva asked calmly.

"Dragon," Rivka muttered with her eyes closed. "You might just have to jump out the window and hope your wings figure it out before we hit the ground."

And a minute later, she had to, because the walls began to crash down around them. As Dragon burst through the open window just before the room was reduced to rubble, all four pairs of eyes — the beast's included — were screwed shut. But they stopped falling, and close to the ground the dragon's wings found a little strength. It was just enough to cushion their landing. Quickly, she transformed back into a horse and galloped away from the exploding pile of debris. Shulamit felt the oddly light bulk of Aviva behind her and leaned back slightly, keeping her safe between her own body and Rivka's. She could feel Rivka's knuckles digging into her back from where she had her arms around Aviva, but it was easier to endure that than think about what would happen if they let Aviva fall.

The horse couldn't go far on the rocky ground, but they managed to make it far enough away that the sorcerer's magic no longer touched the rocks. With her hooves precariously pawing at the uneven ground, she stood in place as Shulamit and Rivka craned their necks around to watch the final destruction of the sorcerer's fortress.

"So that's that," said Rivka flatly, still holding Aviva tightly in both arms since she couldn't very well straddle a horse securely in her condition. "I hope what magic we found will work, because it's all we've got, for now."

"If she can't fly, does that mean we're stuck here?" asked Shulamit.

Rivka nodded. "But I think it's safe to camp. I'm used to the wild, and this is just like any other wild place, with that *schreckliches chazzer* gone." She looked over Aviva with wide eyes and a slowly nodding head. "To think of such a thing—"

"I had to do *something*," said Aviva firmly. "God made many plants and many creatures that taste of death. I merely copied a good defense."

"Like a lantana," Shulamit said, smiling flirtatiously as she played lovingly with Aviva's hair.

Rivka hopped down from the horse. "Come on. Let's set up camp."

Dragon transformed again, and Shulamit and Rivka placed the paralyzed Aviva against the curves of her cool, scaly flesh. "I know you're stone right now, but I'm afraid you'd chip if we set you up against those rocks," Rivka explained.

"Thank you, my lady."

"Please," said Rivka. "I'm no noble. And who said anything about lady?"

"Shulamit called you Rivka."

Rivka huffed. "Okay, fine. But keep it to yourself. I'm Riv." She wandered off suddenly into the distant rocks, her boots crunching on gravel.

"Your new captain is made of thunder," said Aviva. "Now she's going away to rain by herself. She doesn't want to get us wet."

"She has a lot to thunder about," explained Shulamit. "And I don't think she's trying to protect us from what's on her mind. There's something she's ashamed about, and she probably doesn't want to talk about it with anyone." Shulamit was thinking about the things the empty suit of armor said to Rivka back in the fortress, about how her impetuous, almost mindless bravery could have cost her the man to whom she had given her heart.

"How did you meet her?"

Shulamit covered her face with her hand. "There are things *I'm* ashamed about. Oh, Lord, Aviva... the things you missed. Never mind. Your mother's doing better, then?"

"Mostly," said Aviva. "She can walk now — can you believe it? We got her a cane and she can get around everywhere — the fields, the forests, or over to the neighbors' houses to tutor their children. You should have seen her face when we went out to the lake and she was picking ripe sea grapes to eat off the trees, just like in the old days. She can even go to the marketplace with Aba. He's so happy that he can go out and sell his clothing at the market again."

They continued talking until Aviva — who was still recuperating from nearly starving to death — was tired, and Shulamit held her until she fell asleep. Then the queen carefully extricated herself from the tangle of stone woman and scaly dragon flesh and went to find Rivka.

Shulamit walked with quiet steps down the rocks to where Rivka was standing, staring out over the cliff face at a magnificent landscape illuminated by the liquid gold of another sunset. She was careful to announce her presence when she was still a safe distance away, so that Rivka, ever the warrior, wouldn't hear her footfalls and unsheathe her sword in alarm.

Rivka turned to meet her."*Nu*? Is Aviva unwell?"

"She's asleep." Shulamit stepped up beside her to gaze out across the trees in the valley below. "I'm sorry. I know you probably want to be alone right now."

Rivka nodded. "I'm just trying to figure it all out."

"I wish I could be as brave as you are."

"Is it really bravery, though? Or just stupidity? Maybe I'm just too foolish to think of what could go wrong."

"Too much thinking of what could go wrong is what keeps me cowardly," said Shulamit.

"Remember when the crystal ball exploded? There I was, about to put my hands on it. What if it killed us?"

"Remember when Dragon jumped out the window? We all could have died, but it was our only choice. If she had held back and thought about crash-landing, our deaths would have been certain." Shulamit paused.

"The fortress never would have collapsed if I hadn't put the dead man's hand to the wall."

"You didn't know it would do anything bad," Shulamit pointed out. "Don't blame yourself for not thinking of things you had no way of knowing. It's the same with what happened to you up north. You didn't know Isaac was anywhere near your uncle."

"You may be right, little Queenling. How does one as young as you speak such logic?"

"I don't really know anything," said Shulamit, "not really. I just badly need you back, the way you were. You're the strong, confident, brave woman I'm not, and I have so few people to turn to right now."

Rivka's expression softened, and she blinked several times, making the idea flash into Shulamit's mind that she might be holding back tears. "I guess... even if I'm partially to blame for Isaac... and then I couldn't save him... I can only try to make up for it. I can't change it, and I can't stand still in this one spot forever."

"There've been at least two or three Yom Kippurs since all that happened. Haven't you atoned enough?"

"I've forgiven the invaders because they didn't know they were killing an unarmed man. I've forgiven my uncle because he never intended for Isaac to die. But... I've... never even thought about asking for forgiveness for myself. Probably because keeping that guilt helps me hold on to his memory."

"You'll still have all the love you both felt for each other."

"I'd feel like I was disrespecting him."

"He wouldn't want you to feel this way. And he wouldn't want you to have stayed alone so long for his sake."

Rivka's face wrinkled into a cranky scowl. "I'm not saving myself for a memory! I just don't fall in love every five minutes like a lady-in-waiting in some bard's tale."

"I'm sorry. I wasn't thinking." Shulamit looked down. "I know it's not *love*, but I notice women so easily. Even when I was missing Aviva with all my heart, there were the willing women, the statue, the — the make-believe trick woman back there...." *And I approached you, too, that way at least three times*, she added inwardly, glad they were past that.

"That's not how my mind works," said Rivka. "And you know, *Malkeleh*, yes, you're a little girl-crazy, but I can see it's different with Aviva. Now that you're around her, that serious mouth of yours smiles just a little bit more — your eyes open a little wider — you just seem more alive."

128

"I'm so glad we found her in time!" Then Shulamit instantly felt guilty, because Rivka was still alone.

Rivka must have read the frantic expression on her face because she rubbed the queen's shoulder affectionately and replied, "Be happy — don't worry about me. Remember, there are plenty of real men who are career warriors and remain single. It's only on a woman that being unmarried looks odd. Like those men, I've got plenty of other things to do." She smiled slightly. "Not many can brag of triumphs and adventures like mine."

Shulamit took her hand and squeezed it comfortingly. "He would be *so* proud of you."

The warrior sighed heavily. "It's dark. We should go back to Aviva."

❀ • ❀ • ❀

As Rivka followed the queen back to the sleeping dragon, she was surprised to realize that she actually did feel a little bit better. Maybe it was just allowing herself to think of Isaac that had lightened her mood. Even all these years later, picturing his face or imagining his voice made her feel as if she were full of bubbles. They might be bubbles of searing hot pain at this point, but they still filled her and made her whole.

There was also a beautiful new feeling growing within her as she slowly realized that for the first time in her life, a young person looked up to her and depended on her. So she vowed to honor her dead by being the strong woman Isaac would have been proud to see, and honor her living by being the strong woman Shulamit needed.

The next day, Shulamit awoke to find Rivka doing physical exercises around the rocks. "You're full of energy this morning."

"I had a great dream," said Rivka, and she turned a cartwheel.

Shulamit's eyebrows lifted. "Must have been some dream. I've never been able to move around like that."

"I dreamed about marrying Isaac," Rivka told her, practically bouncing off the rocks.

"When I wake up from good dreams I'm sad," Aviva observed. "Often as a child I'd dream that Ima was well again, and then when I woke up and realized she was still in bed, it would crush me."

"It's different when someone dies," Shulamit explained. "I'm happy to dream of my father, because I miss him and that way I get to see him again."

"What was the wedding like?" Aviva asked.

"I was wearing a fancy dress from my people, and he was in his cassock. We were standing in the empty room back there in the fortress — the room we figured was intended to trap the enlightened? Anyway, you performed the ceremony"— she pointed at Shulamit — "and my mother was there, and she didn't think my dress had enough jewels on it. And I kept worrying about whether or not I had bathed." She let out a ribald chuckle, flushing.

Dragon flapped her wings. A powerful wind swirled up around the three women.

"She can fly again!" Shulamit clapped her hands and jumped up and down. "To the holy house!"

"I'm thinking two days. We can leave now, if you're willing to eat breakfast while we ride."

Dragon lifted the three of them into the air as they passed old goat meat and tangerines between themselves.

❀ • ❀ • ❀

They spent the next two days in flight, and Aviva entertained them with colorful renditions of the folktales of the region. When she had exhausted her supply, Shulamit picked up the conversational reins with memories of her father, and Rivka talked of her years in battle fighting in this or that war for this or that king. When they camped again by the lake, they gathered more tangerines for the rest of the journey.

It was nightfall on the second day when they finally reached the holy house. Tamar was standing in the doorway reciting her evening prayer at the moon when the three women, followed by Dragon in her horse form, entered the garden. "Good evening," Rivka called out.

"You've returned, my son! I hope you are well, Your Majesty. Have you been victorious? And who is this?" The old woman hobbled toward them with her arms outstretched in welcome.

Rivka removed the crystal vial from where she had hidden it in her clothing. "Is this the curse blight?"

"Yes!" Tamar beamed. But then she squinted at the bottle. "But, my son, the bottle is empty!"

Rivka bit her lip. "Well, yes. But we have an idea. Actually, it was the queen's idea." She held out her hand toward Shulamit.

131

"If we put the vial deep into the holy water, and then Riv here breaks the front of the vessel, the water will flow down into the courtyard and free everyone at once." Shulamit's eyes were fixed with nervous intensity on Tamar, and Rivka hoped along with her that her suggestion would go over well.

"But... the holy water..."

"Needs to be put to practical use," Shulamit pointed out. She took Tamar's hands in hers. "We must save lives, Sister."

Tamar nodded solemnly. "Yes, we must." Then she noticed Aviva again. "This woman is stone, and yet not all stone!"

"He died before he could finish the curse," Aviva explained.

Tamar's eyes widened. "Then the sorcerer is dead?"

They explained how the sorcerer died, and how his death and the drought within the bottle were part of the same tale.

"It's too dark to do this work now," said Tamar. "I was just about to prepare myself for sleep. Do you wish to sleep upon the roof again?"

"Your Majesty, why don't you and Aviva take a room inside the temple for tonight," Rivka suggested. It had occurred to her that the lovers hadn't been alone, not *truly*, since their reunion, and she wanted to engineer an opportunity to give them privacy — even if Aviva was still made out of stone. With any luck, she'd be transformed tomorrow, and then they'd spend another night with the same sleeping arrangements without attracting undue attention. "Now that you have company, and that the sorcerer's no longer a threat, I hope you feel safer without me guarding you."

To be honest, she also relished the idea of a night to herself. When Tamar and the girls had finally gone to bed, she curled up against Dragon's comforting muscles and fell asleep as if blown out like a candle.

❀ • ❀ • ❀

"Answering, Esther said: if I find favor in your eyes, if the king judges it to be good, then grant to me my soul and my people, in answer to my plea," Shulamit read, her voice rising dramatically. The only thing she'd found in the temple to read were religious stories, which didn't surprise her, but that was okay. Even in the mass of male-centered, violent tales, she could still find something that resonated with her.

Aviva listened intently from her position of forced repose on the bed in the modest cell Tamar had given them for the duration of their stay. Her head was propped up against what cushions Shulamit had managed to scrounge, and now a loose lock of hair had floated into her face. She attempted unsuccessfully to blow it away. "My hair sticks are gone, aren't they?"

Shulamit looked up from the book and grimaced. "Yeah, sorry — I think you were wearing them when we found you, but then the fortress collapsed and Dragon was flying sideways—" She reached out a trembling hand and brushed Aviva's hair back out of her face. Heat coursed through her body at the intimate contact, but she mentally slapped herself because the sensation felt like taking advantage, given Aviva's condition.

"Shulamit?" Aviva was looking up at her with large, questioning eyes.

"Hmm?"

"If the power of that moon-juice died with the sorcerer," Aviva said in a heartfelt voice, "or if the magic runs out and there isn't enough for me—"

Shulamit instinctively tried to take Aviva's hands in hers, but then jolted at the feeling of cold stone against her palms. She

133

looked into her eyes. "I'll still take you back to the palace and keep reading to you. Although you'll probably have to put up with things like *Kefir the Younger's Observations on Stalagmites* until I can find some good fiction for you. You know what kinds of things I usually read!"

"I've always admired that about you — that you want to know *everything* about your kingdom, even the rocks and plants." Aviva's eyes glittered. "That wasn't what I was going to ask, but I'll gladly come along. I was going to offer to teach. Even if I can't hatch out of my egg, I can instruct others. I just need a little help building the trellis — I can grow my own vine."

Shulamit exhaled. "Sometimes I can't even fathom your generosity."

"Then stop fathoming and get back to reading!" Aviva stuck her tongue out at her.

"You just want me to say the bad guy's name again so you can go back to making silly noises to drown it out."

"And *you* only picked this story because you have honey in your heart for Queen Esther."

"I guess I have high standards, then," Shulamit shot back, and returned to squinting at the book in the flickering lantern light.

❀ • ❀ • ❀

The sun arose on the morning of the magic and bathed the temple in radiance. Shulamit brought breakfast up to Rivka and Dragon on the roof. "I carried Aviva out into the garden so she can be healed with everybody else. I can't believe how light she is, even though she's made of rock."

"Already in a week you're stronger — now you can carry a grown woman!" Rivka chuckled.

"A grown woman made of pumice," Shulamit amended. "I think that's what they call very light rocks. I read about it in a book on gems. At least she didn't get turned to gold!"

Rivka, munching on rice, looked out over the courtyard. "Where's Tamar?"

"Down there." Shulamit pointed. "She wants to be ready to greet her afflicted sisters when they return to life."

"Beautiful day for them to wake up to. Hey! Where're you going?" For Dragon had flapped her wings and lifted off the roof. She landed in the courtyard and returned to her horse form. Rivka soon had her answer as the mare began to graze heartily. "Breakfast time for everyone."

"I hope Tamar made enough food for the rest of her flock. If not, if any of them are hungry when they come back to life, we'll have to work fast!"

Rivka took out the nearly empty crystal vial and placed it deep within the center of the calm still pool of holy water.

Shulamit stared down after it, sunlight glinting painfully into her eyes. Impulsively, she dipped one hand into the basin and then cooled her face with the water.

Rivka gave her a sharp glance. "What are you doing?"

Shulamit turned to look at her. "I know I'm not cursed. But if I didn't *try*, I'd feel silly later. Just in case." What would it be like to be able to eat challah again? Or enjoy the savory tanginess of chicken roasted with lemon and herbs?

"Poor Queenling!" Then a change came over Rivka's face. For a moment, she stood still, staring at the edge of the basin and centering her physical strength. Next, she unsheathed her sword.

Shulamit watched her in impressed awe as the warrior held her sword in both hands, pointed in the air. Rivka was breathing deeply. She might even have been praying.

Shulamit prayed too. The fingers of each hand, down at her side, separated into the hand position that looked like her initial, shin. ש *Shekhinah*, feminine of God. *Female strength, do not fail us today.*

Rivka raised her sword.

Far away in the courtyard, Tamar looked up at her expectantly.

Down came the blade with a dull *bang*.

The clay chipped.

Rivka hacked away at the edge of the basin nearest the roof's edge, until finally a fissure formed. "You're doing it! It's working!" Shulamit exclaimed, her eyes sparkling.

Again and again Rivka brought her sword down upon the basin, until finally, a chunk came free. Water began to flow. But it wasn't enough. "Faster!"

Rivka hammered away, until finally—

Splash went the water, carrying away pieces of broken basin with it. The holy water poured down from the roof, draining the broken basin entirely. It flowed into the courtyard, soaking each and every statue, including Aviva — not to mention Tamar and the horse.

Shulamit watched as color returned to the flesh of the statues. No more were they cold gray; a rich, healthy golden-brown flooded each woman from head to toe. Their simple robes returned to the brilliant mango color of the turmeric that had dyed them, and their hair was once more soft and black. It was incredible. She beheld Aviva stand up of her own accord, and she held out her arms to her beloved. "Aviva!"

Aviva came tripping up the center path toward the temple. "Shulamit! Oh..."

"Don't hurt yourself," Shulamit admonished her.

Tamar was toddling around between the women, greeting them with tearful, smiling hugs.

Then Shulamit noticed something she hadn't anticipated. Something was happening to the horse. She had been standing somewhere at the side of the courtyard, but she, too, was transforming — and not in a way they'd ever seen before.

"Rivka? Look at Dragon — she's — the curse blight is working on her too! She's not really a horse!" And as Shulamit kept watching, she could barely believe her eyes. The horse's body was rapidly shrinking into that of a human's — and — "She's not really a *she*!"

The queen clapped her hands to her face as the man crouching on the ground, where the horse had been, straightened his posture and stood to face the roof. He was stocky, tall, and lighter-skinned, like Rivka, with a broad chest and shoulders, muscular arms, and a bit of a stomach. His dark-blond hair was cropped short, and his impish eyes looked up at them from beneath pointed eyebrows on a round face.

Shulamit wheeled around to face the warrior beside her. "Rivka?"

"*Isaac?!*"

Chapter 16: Has the Dragon a Heart?

One by one, the nuns began to notice the naked man in their midst. Some drew back in fright; others giggled, or hid their faces. Others merely pointed and murmured to those nearest. A few of them, the braver ones who had stood up to the sorcerer, charged toward him with their hand clasped into fists.

"Do not harm him!" Rivka shouted down from the roof. She stood there, as still as a statue herself holding her sword at her side. Finally, the impulsive warrior had encountered a moment that required her to wait and see before acting.

Shulamit, ever the intellectual, couldn't help peering down at the unclothed wizard. Since she had most recently known him as a female horse, she was relieved — for Rivka's sake, of course — to discover that no damage remained from the years without his own body. He may have been a mare, but now he was — well, an ordinary human male, with all the usual parts restored.

The visibility of those parts was causing a commotion amid the celibate holy women. Finally, one of them removed the headscarf that covered her hair and handed it to him.

He nodded to her in thanks. As she withdrew from him, he knotted it around his waist. Then he held his arms up to the sky.

"Hail this luminous day!" he bellowed, his northern accent a bit stronger than Rivka's. His piercing blue gaze was fixed directly on Rivka, who watched him from the roof, breathing heavily but otherwise still. "And the hero who awakened me?"

Slowly, Rivka raised the arm that held her sword. The steel glinted in the sunlight.

"Mighty Riv," Isaac began, his voice this time slightly more cajoling, even slithering, "may I beg of you the fragment of cloth that you wear beneath your helmet? I'm unclothed and I don't want these good women should turn back to stone if they look upon me." A mischievous smile followed his words.

"It's only—" Well, of *course* he knew what it was! He'd been there the whole time! Without another word, Rivka took off her helmet and unpeeled the charred cassock fragment from her unruly blonde hair. She threw it down into the courtyard, where Aviva caught it and carried it over to the wizard.

He accepted it and manipulated it a few times, tossing it around and around as if trying to find something. With each turn, the fabric grew in his hands until soon it had become a full-sized cassock again. He wrapped it around himself and fastened all the closures, until he stood before Rivka just as he once had, far away in their northern homeland.

Then he lifted his head and spoke once more to the stunned woman on the rooftop.

"Mighty One," he began. "Three years ago my Wizard Order cursed me into the form of a mare, and I thank you for freeing me from that curse. It was a punishment intended to shame me. Thinking that I had already broken my vows, they declared them forfeit and cast me from the Order. They thought I devised new enchantments to obscure my activities with a certain lady, when they were mistaken and I never broke my vows at all. Now that I'm free of both the curse and of my vows, I ask of you now—"

Rivka listened, obviously entranced and trembling slightly—

"Do you know where I might find that lady, and if she still feels as she did when she spoke intimately with her queen about me? Because, while I'd be perfectly content to ride with you and fight alongside you until the day I *truly* die, if that lady is willing, now that I'm free, I would beg of her the privilege of becoming her husband."

Rivka's voice rang out loud and clear down from the temple roof. "I know that lady, and she still loves you. She thought you were dead, but she never met a man worthy of succeeding you. She will *absolutely* marry you. There are things that fire cannot destroy." Rivka paused. "Speaking of which, how are you alive?! I'm so glad to see you, but I'm completely *fartumult*!"

"I will show you. Behold—" And Isaac, raising his arms in the air, transformed back into the dragon form. The holy sisters scattered in awe and pointed and stared as he flew up to the rooftop to join his warrior bride.

As soon as he was safely on the roof, he returned to human form — still in the cassock, Shulamit noted. She had to crane her head upward to look at him — he was even taller than Rivka, even if by only a few inches, and his broadness and height were startling and majestic like a baobab tree. "So..." She put her finger to her jawline and tapped it a few times thoughtfully. "The dragon form is one of your magical abilities, and not part of the curse?"

"Exactly, Your Majesty. The curse robbed me of most of my abilities and even my humanity. The power to transform into a dragon was the only thing I had left — and even that, they managed to weaken. You will find that my flight won't tire now as it once did — at least, not as easily."

"Oh, Isaac," was all Rivka could say, her breathing both deep and rapid.

"Why did they leave you with that?" asked Shulamit curiously.

"They'd nearly finished the curse when the attack began," the wizard explained. "My Order — my *ex*-Order, that is — they didn't want to get tangled up in the middle of the baron's feuding. Leaving me as I was, they fled for the mountains. They, uh, had *better* things to do."

"Just like Aviva!"

"So you flew out of the building before the second floor exploded?" Rivka's eyes were moving back and forth, as if she were putting the pieces together.

"I saw you jump out the window," said Isaac. "My intention was to fly over and join you, but after being drugged by the baron, my wings failed nearly instantly. I was a horse again before you came up for air, and then one of those *paskudnyaks* from Apple Valley was on my back."

"The other wizards really thought you'd — that you and I had—" Rivka flushed, and she wiped sweat from her face underneath the mask.

"The messenger mentioned you being there when he was taking down the baron's words," Isaac explained. "That was all it took, because honestly, they wouldn't believe that the baron's anger had nothing to do with anyone being seduced and deflowered. They knew what happened to your mother, and how it irritated the baron. When they woke me to berate me and cast me out, I protested that I never laid with you — I never laid with anybody in my life — and if we did anything against their arbitrary rules, they would have seen it, with all the enchantments watching over me. All they did was laugh and say I came up with a way to hide it from them. They stripped me, beat me up..."

"Horrible. I wish I'd known you were with me all along..."

"I had no way of telling you," said Isaac sadly. "A real dragon's mind can't understand written language, so I couldn't scratch it into the dirt with my claws, and when I was a mare, as part of the curse, I had a mare's mind, which was even worse. Yet, somehow, even as a mare, I still knew that I loved you... I just didn't know who you were, or what that meant." Then he turned to face Shulamit. "Your Majesty, you are, without a doubt, one of the most intelligent young women I've ever been lucky enough to meet. You read encyclopedias for fun. Surely your great brain can think of a reason not to be up here right now?"

It has been said that sometimes the intellect and the common sense do not necessarily occupy the same skull at the same time. Shulamit grinned with shame, then nodded. "I'm sorry. I'll go down to Aviva. Um," she added as she started for the stairs, "nice to meet you."

❀ • ❀ • ❀

Rivka carefully sheathed her sword, unable to tear her eyes from the man before her. There were so many more questions she wanted to ask him; confidences to tell him; shared adventures to discuss. Three years of conversations they might have had burst forth from her mind at once, vying for fruition like dogs scrambling to be first on a bone. She gazed over those features she remembered so well. He was a ghost made real, a cherished memory now flesh that rose and fell with every breath, with eyes that blinked in the glare of the tropical sun and lips that twitched up subtly at the edges to smile at her, just as she'd remembered.

Now he was talking to her just as in her dreams, instead of his heavily accented Perachi. "I'm sorry I eavesdropped on your private conversations with the queen," Isaac told Rivka in their native language. "Of course, it's not as if I had a choice."

"I need no privacy from you, Isaac," said Rivka, her eyes growing heavy-lidded and her voice confident. "I want *less* privacy from you."

Isaac smirked. "I should remind you that I've seen you bathing."

"I saw *you* down in the courtyard." Rivka was still digesting the fact that she'd gone from living in a reality where he had died years ago to seeing him naked within the span of forty-five seconds. Her body tingled, and the daylight felt even hotter than usual. "I never knew you could turn into a dragon."

142

Isaac nodded. "Dragons and other general serpent-type creatures. I'll explain it all later. The night the door stood between us, that's how I was able to get through the passageways unmolested. Didn't you wonder why you heard no footsteps as I approached? It was a lizard who wooed you that night. I stood on the door itself."

"A lizard!" She pictured what he must have looked like, his red dewlap pushing in and out, and shook her head with the sheer unexpectedness of it all. "It's still strange to hear you talk openly of wooing."

"Would it be strange if I touched you?" His voice had turned to chocolate.

"Very strange. And very delicious."

One of his hands took one of hers. Despite sleeping against him almost every night, this was the first time she had knowingly touched him. Her fingers grabbed at him hungrily, and she drew closer, eager for more.

"Mind yourself, *Riv*. You don't want to shatter the carefully constructed conceit I concocted down there."

"I'm glad you said those things," said Rivka. "Not just to keep my secret, but also because I knew instantly that you were no mind-reading trick like the suits of armor in the sorcerer's keep. Absolutely nothing in my own mind would have produced such sly cleverness. I'm far too straightforward for that."

"You always have been. It's one of the reasons I love you." He moved closer, then quickly stopped and glanced down into the courtyard at the holy women. With a growl, he added, "Would that I had you alone."

His tone was so unexpected that Rivka moaned out loud before she realized what she was doing. Then she turned her head

143

quickly. "There's the stairwell. The women are all occupied downstairs."

"And if they come upon us?"

"We're both warriors. We'll know if anyone approaches."

Bustling each other into the stairwell with the excitement of frolicking kittens, the warrior and the wizard disappeared from view.

From the moment his lips touched hers, her blood turned to wine and the wine into liquid fire. Both his hands were clasped firmly on her biceps, holding her body close to his. She wrapped every available limb around him, exploring wonderful unfamiliar territory with curious fingers. Now she was pressed against the wall, and he broke away from the kiss to nuzzle a trail with his mouth across her throat. Pushing aside leather armor, he tasted the side of her neck.

In between gasps of pleasure, she murmured throatily, "Isaac... mind your sword!"

"Why, do you mind it?"

"Hardly."

"That's two of those. You said you weren't — ahhh! — sly and clever. Maybe my sense of humor is rubbing off on you."

Rivka gasped again, craving him with an intensity bordering on pain. "I'm sorry. I don't have any more. You win."

"What do I win?"

"Many adventure stories begin with a dragon who carries off a virgin."

"Those same stories end with the dragon being conquered by a warrior."

"Oh, if we're not married soon I shall gnaw off my own head!"

"Marry me now." He took both her hands in his. "Can't Queen Shulamit help us?"

"What, really? Like in my dream?"

"In some countries the monarch has that power."

"I'm going to go ask her." Rivka broke away from him, but he pulled her back by one hand.

"One more kiss."

"Oh...."

Eventually, Rivka managed to get downstairs and into the courtyard. Isaac followed her, so the holy women wouldn't get nervous about having two strange men in the temple by themselves.

She found Shulamit seated next to Aviva, who was lying down on the ground being examined by the very woman whom Shulamit had first admired in statue form. "Riv! Guess what? It turns out that Keren is trained in healing arts. She's going to take care of Aviva while we're here and make sure she gets her strength back."

Rivka smiled. "I know we just banished you," she said in a low murmur, "but could you come back up to the roof for a moment? Isaac thinks you have... a certain privilege, as a head of state."

Shulamit understood instantly, and one hand flew to her mouth with happy surprise. "Oh! I—I don't know the words yet."

"Do they matter?"

"I guess not." She took Aviva's hand. "I'll be back. Queen stuff."

Aviva smiled back at her and then returned to answering Keren's questions about how each part of her body felt from the period of starvation and dehydration.

Shulamit and Rivka joined Isaac, who was waiting for them at the door to the temple. "She'll do it," said Rivka, "but she doesn't know the words."

"I won't hold it against her. She's got plenty of time to learn them later for other people."

The three of them clambered back up the stairs to the roof.

"Wait! I know one thing!" Shulamit bent down and reached into the wreckage of the holy water basin to pluck out the now completely empty crystal vial that had held the curse blight. "For him to step on."

She put it on the ground between herself and the impatient lovers, then stood straight up and blinked a few times. "Isaac of the Wizards and Rivka bat Beet-greens... oh, I'm so sorry, you should never have told me that. It stuck in my head, and now it came out because I'm flustered."

"Forget it," said Rivka, laughing. "I'm about to marry Isaac. Do you really think I care?"

Shulamit smiled with relief.

"It should be 'daughter of *Bitter*-greens', anyway," Isaac suggested. "Isn't your mother called Miriam?"

"Riv Maror," Rivka mused. She lifted one eyebrow. "I like it!"

"I like it too — I think it's really clever," Shulamit agreed. "If I had to think of a food that was bold and assertive like you are, horseradish is a good one! Anyway: Isaac and Rivka — may God bless you both with a lifetime of shared love, and may He forgive me for improvising. Wait — don't we need a ketubah?"

146

"I promise to keep saving your life," said Isaac directly to Rivka.

"I promise to keep giving you reasons to want to," said Rivka back to him. They were both beaming.

"Since I can't remember what else to say — you're married now. Have a good life together. Oh, and the glass!"

With one stomp of her boot, Rivka smashed the thing to powder.

Isaac lifted his pointed eyebrows and smiled his impish smile, and Shulamit burst into giggles.

"What's going on up there?" called a voice from the courtyard. One of the sisters was looking up at them curiously.

"Your Majesty, please send the warrior down so that we may thank him!" called another. "He's too shy. We must have a feast!"

"Though our fare is humble, we're indeed grateful and wish to repay you both," spoke a third. "We thought he was coming down to receive his honors, but then you both went back up to the roof."

Isaac transformed back into a dragon and gave the two women a lift straight into the midst of the crowd.

Chapter 17: Sharing the Treasure

There was a great celebration, and the holy women played instruments and sang and danced for the four of them. When they knew the songs and dances, they joined in. Eventually, everybody wore themselves out and sat down on the ground to feast. Some of the women carried low, wooden tables out to the courtyard and spread the meal out across them. The food was simple, but there was enough to go around.

The two northerners spoke quietly in their own language while they ate. "The night when we were together and you were a lizard," Rivka asked, "you still spoke as a man. Sang to me, even. When you were a dragon these past three years, couldn't you speak and identify yourself?"

Isaac shook his head. "I was under too many curses. Sometimes it was hard to remember human language at all. That's why my first words to you today were in their language." He cocked his head toward the bevy of Perachis. "It's all I've been hearing lately."

"I wish you'd told me about your serpent powers," said Rivka, "so I had a chance of guessing it was you all along."

"I made a lot of decisions based on what I thought was best. One of them was not telling anyone more than I thought they needed to know — even you. I'm so sorry about that." He gazed deeply into her eyes. "Even befriending you was a decision made from arrogance — I thought, with the celibacy vow, it wouldn't matter if I was friends with a woman, because — woman, man, everyone is the same if you're chaste and not supposed to love any of them. And maybe it would have worked out that way — if the woman had been anyone but you, Mighty One." At these last words, his eyebrows reached for her and Rivka had to wipe sweat off her face beneath her cloth mask. She wanted to touch him so badly it made her rib cage ache, but she looked away and ate another mouthful of rice instead.

When everyone was finished with the main meal, some of the holy women produced mangoes and litchis. As they peeled fruit and relaxed in the shade of the palm trees, the women listened to Isaac and Riv's stories of adventure and combat. They heard the story of the injury to Isaac's right hand (during which Isaac managed to accidentally start a rumor that Riv's cloth mask hid an even more grisly and disfiguring scar), and of their joint capture of the famous twin brothers who had robbed so many travelers in the lands just north of them. So raptly did the warriors' tales hold their attention that nobody noticed when the sky grew silver and the air alive with dead leaves.

And so the rain started up too quickly to avoid, and many of them were drenched as they scurried about clearing away dishes and tables and gathering up the piles of pits and peels to throw away. By the time everyone had bustled everything safely inside the temple, a gloriously heavy shower was pelting the courtyard.

Tamar toddled toward Isaac and Rivka, holding a lit lamp. "My sons, you'll be more comfortable drying off in our private meditation room. Come." She led them down the hall, and Rivka shot a shocked look at Isaac, barely able to believe their luck.

"I'm sure she's trying to keep our male eyes away from her holy women's clinging wet robes," Isaac murmured in barely audible northern tongue. Rivka smirked.

Tamar opened a big, heavy door at the end of a hallway and showed them inside a room decorated with simple curtains designed to induce inner peace. "You'll need this lamp — there are no windows." She set the lamp down on the floor and stepped back into the hallway. "Come out when you've dried off your clothes, and we'll be waiting in the main hall. Thank you for all your stories. We enjoyed that so much!"

"And thank you for the food," said Rivka.

"Don't be alarmed if you hear heavy footsteps or thumping," Isaac piped up. "We may spar to pass the time."

Rivka stifled a laugh.

"Enjoy yourselves, my sons!" Tamar turned and started her slow walk back down the hallway.

Rivka closed the big wooden door and carefully made sure it was latched as sturdily as possible. Then she turned around, and burst into laughter as she beheld not Isaac the man, but a large python, as big around as her thigh in some places, slithering toward her. Its scales were a mottled yellow-and-cream color like rich pasture-fed butter, and its tongue flickered in and out of its mouth as it sniffed for her. Of course, at this point, she knew who he was.

She could also see Isaac's wet cassock on the other side of the room draped over a stone bench.

The snake glided across the floor and then began to climb up her left leg. As its squeezing muscles wrapped around her, she couldn't help quivering with pleasure, her back thrown against the door. "Stop showing off," she commanded. "I know I married a traveling menagerie, but right now I want my husband as a human."

"At once," said Isaac's voice from *somewhere*, and then the snake dropped in a coil on the floor in front of her. He rose up again in human form and seized her in his arms. She caressed the massive bulk of his back and shoulders, kissing him, lifting her chin as he breathed fire across her throat like the dragon he was. His good hand was underneath her soaked tunic fumbling at the cord between the legs of her trousers, opening them to the air, and then his fingers brushed her skin directly.

Once more, Rivka had her back to a door and was moaning over love and desire for Isaac the wizard, but this time he was on the right side of that door — pinning her to its surface, holding her,

150

and now joining with her. She stood with her legs wide and her arms around him, clutching at him and pressing him closer. Like a river overflowing its banks, ardor and relief poured from her heart and made her feel as if she were floating. Isaac was in her arms at last.

When the room stopped spinning, a panting, somewhat sweaty man rested his head in the soft place between her neck and her shoulder, his nose buried in her skin. "Who is this brave woman," he said softly between gasps, "who has pierced my heart?"

Rivka smiled, at peace, and held him.

She was still wearing her sword.

❀ • ❀ • ❀

When Rivka and Isaac's clothing had dried enough to wear comfortably they emerged from their chrysalis, taking the lamp with them. They found the rest of the holy women scattered throughout the temple, mostly reading peacefully, but some cleaning or praying or working at various crafts. Aviva sat against the wall on a cushion made from something coarse and green, with her hands massaging Shulamit's head, which lay in her lap.

There was something suspicious about the position of Shulamit's body, and Rivka quickened her pace as she approached them. "Is everything okay?"

"Everyone else bites pita, but with my darling, the pita bites back," said Aviva.

Rivka lifted an eyebrow. "Shula, what did you—"

"I just wanted to see if the curse antidote had cured me."

151

"She just ate a bite or two, so it's only stomach cramps, thank God," Aviva explained. "But I couldn't even get her to a bed."

"Sorry." Rivka poked the queen's shoulder affectionately. "I can carry you somewhere more comfortable."

"I'll be all right," Shulamit said weakly. "I'm used to this." She drew her knees up closer to her chest. "Aviva didn't want to let me, but if I didn't try, I'd never know."

"Do you need anything?"

"Water might help," Shulamit mumbled.

Rivka and Isaac ran off in search.

❀ • ❀ • ❀

"I'm so happy you're here to take care of me again," said Shulamit, burying her face in Aviva's lap. "Losing you hurt worse than these cramps."

"I hurt myself too," Aviva reminded her. "I just couldn't think of anything but how I owe my mother my life, and..." She hugged the girl in her lap.

"But we could have figured out a way to make *everybody* happy — maybe not honestly, but Nathan was a wicked criminal and he deserved to be tricked." Shulamit winced with pain, and when the wave of squeezing in her gut had subsided, she continued. "What's more, I want you in my life, by my side, forever, but now I'm scared that the next time you're in trouble you'll run away again and I won't know anything about it. My brain runs and runs around in circles and keeps thinking of all these perfectly logical reasons that you wouldn't want to be around me, except they're really probably silly—"

152

"What do you want?"

"I—"

"I want you to feel safe. I'm sorry about the way I did things before, and I want to make sure I do better."

"Now I feel ashamed. What you did for your mother was wonderful. I don't think I have that kind of strength."

"I need to know what will make you feel safe."

"Just please — promise me that you'll tell me things from now on. If you need money, if someone threatens your family, anything. Owww..." Shulamit breathed heavily for a few seconds. "Whatever it is, we can — tackle it together.

"I promise."

"In any case, my father's money paid for your mother's operation, so I'm glad at least to know the money went somewhere good."

Isaac and Rivka returned with the water, and Shulamit drank deeply and rested.

That night before dinner, Keren examined the queen and determined that it was safe for her to eat again, and even that her wrist sprain was healing up quickly. She also declared that Aviva had recovered fully from her ordeal back at the fortress. The two ate heartily and then prepared for bed in the room in which they had slept the night before.

Only, this time there would be no Book of Esther, only their own version of the Song of Songs. Tonight would be a sanctified reunion of hands and bodies and dreams and sighs. This night would be the warmhearted self-satisfaction of knowing that you had brought her pleasure, and the sweet gratefulness of your own pleasure under her touches.

They eventually dozed off, but as appealing as it sounds to fall asleep tangled up with another person without any clothes on, sometimes your arm falls asleep or they breathe on you funny and the situation may be more comfortable in the heart than it is on the limbs. Shulamit woke up again while it was still dark. She felt sticky and stale from falling asleep sweaty. In her effort to extricate the arm that had fallen asleep from beneath Aviva's body, she inadvertently woke her up. "Mmm," Aviva mumbled. "Your face smells of flowers."

She wasn't talking about the ones that grew on trees.

Shulamit grinned awkwardly. "Yours too. We should probably go out to the creek in the back of the temple and clean up before we present ourselves to anybody."

"Good idea," said Aviva, still groggy. The only movement she made was to plant a hand on each of Shulamit's hips and pull her back on top of her.

"Well, since we haven't bathed *yet*..." Shulamit murmured, and slithered down in between Aviva's legs.

When, as Aviva phrased it, "the soft little kittens had finished meowing," the girls put their clothing back on and made their way to the back of the temple as best they could without being seen. They dodged two women who were on breakfast duty and a third who was doing the cleaning, holding themselves flat against the wall and moving in shadows, all while trying their hardest not to giggle. Finally they were outside, in a quiet gray world of predawn mist. Birdcalls rang from distant trees, preparing the way for the inevitable sunrise.

Rivka was already in the water, scrubbing away her own trophies. "She's glowing," Aviva whispered, giggling. "I bet she can even understand the birds." Then she raised her voice. "Good morning, Riv! What are the birds singing about today?"

154

The warrior raised her eyebrows in amusement and waved to them. "They're saying it's good you two are up. We can get an early start. We'll stay in Ir Ilan tonight, but we'll have to make it to the marketplace in time to get Shulamit her dinner."

"Where's Isaac?" asked Shulamit.

Rivka cocked her head upward. "He went back to sleep."

Shulamit and Aviva looked up and saw the snoozing dragon on the rooftop. "So, we can fly on his back the whole time on the way home?" Shulamit asked as they removed their clothing and entered the water.

Rivka nodded. "His stamina will be much better now that we've lifted the curse."

"But you won't have a horse anymore."

Rivka smirked at her. "Guess I'll only have a dragon!"

"And a husband," Shulamit pointed out. "We should be home by tomorrow night. Then I can send Nathan away and put you in his place. His crime doesn't fit his position."

"Will the rest of the guards resent me if I displace him so suddenly?" Rivka asked.

"There's something neither of you know," said Aviva. "Each time King Noach gave him more money to increase the wages of the guards, Nathan told himself it would be permissible, just this once, to keep it for himself — because of his growing family."

Shulamit's eyes were once again saucers. "How did you find out?"

"He sent his older sons with the money in the bag to pay the surgeons directly, when they treated Ima," said Aviva. "I was thrown together with them a bit during the ordeal. They liked me a little too much, and it was hard to get away from them.

Remember what I said about my bosom. Anyway, I encouraged them to flirt with the Lady Wine instead of me, and they told her many secrets that I had the benefit of overhearing. Lady Wine knows everyone's secrets."

"When I'm drunk, I just sing louder," Rivka muttered. "So if I pay them the wages they deserve—"

"Besides, they've already heard of your reputation," Shulamit pointed out. "They hired you to rescue me from the kidnappers."

"Some of my captures — as a bounty hunter — are a bit well-known, to those in the trade," Rivka acceded.

"How did you get the job at the bawdy house, before you had all your war experience?" Shulamit asked. "I mean, I know Isaac had taught you how to swordfight, and you'd been in the one battle back home, but you weren't, you know, *the mighty Riv* yet."

"I was staying there as a guest — it was also an inn — mostly just keeping to myself so I could practice with my sword, except when I was looking for odd jobs to earn money. And one night, one of the customers tried to attack one of the willing women. Seems he was, uh, having some trouble."

"His leaves had wilted," Aviva supplied helpfully.

"Exactly. Anyway, he blamed Raizel for his own deficiencies, and things got violent. I heard the commotion and the screaming and grabbed my sword. He ended up tossed out the window into a pile of rotting kitchen scrapings. I threw his luggage out after him, after taking out Raizel's fee."

"I wish I could have seen that," said Shulamit admiringly.

"The rest of the willing women were clustered in the hallway at that point, and they'd all seen what happened. They pretty much demanded that I stay on as their guard. Shayna — the madam — her lover had walked out on her and he'd been the guard before me. That's why they didn't have anyone to protect them that night. So I agreed to stay on. Of course, a few of them found it necessary to insist that I understand their rule against the guard making free with their services. You've known me for only a week or two but you've already seen how direct I am — and this was the middle of the night, only weeks after I thought I'd lost Isaac and left the only home I'd ever known. I simply opened my shirt, and said that I had a pair of my own and wasn't interested, so they didn't have to worry."

Shulamit wilted.

"I'm sorry, Queenling," Rivka added. "I wasn't really thinking about women like you two. To be honest I'm not sure I knew it existed at that point."

Shulamit's expression softened, and then broke into a smile. "And then, despite all your talk of loving only men, you spent three years loving a soul imprisoned inside a female body."

"I knew you weren't going to let that alone." Rivka splashed her in the face, then quickly got out of the water and started pulling on her clothing. "Better get dressed before the holy women see all this and bust up my cover."

Shulamit grinned. "Right before I met you, I was thinking that I wanted to fire all my guards and replace them with men who were like Aviva and me. Now, with you and Isaac around, that's what you're going to look like."

"*Feh*," Rivka said with a shrug. "I've got Isaac back, and I'm about to start my dream job. Plus, I'm good at what I do! So the rest doesn't matter."

❀ • ❀ • ❀

Rivka walked away a little distance into the trees, giving the girls some privacy. Gazing back at the temple, Rivka could see the black-green of her husband still asleep in dragon form on the roof. She felt overwhelmed by joy, and clasped a paper to her breast.

In the golden light of sunrise, she reread the words to which she'd awoken.

My beloved, my wife, my Mighty One—

You've fallen asleep (and no wonder, considering our exertions!) but I can't sleep just yet — I'm still getting used to being myself again, and my mind is too active. So I snuck downstairs to find paper and ink and now I'm writing to you, with my clumsy left hand just as I did all those years ago when you were borrowing my books.

The morning you left your uncle's castle, I carried you away in a mix of sorrow and joy — I had lost most of my human faculties, but I was also filled with elation that we were together, fighting as we'd dreamed. You wept for me, and told me things about myself without knowing to whom you spoke. I was flattered and it felt good to hear it, but I quickly worked out a plan to reveal myself to you.

As soon as we'd gotten beyond the forest, you told me to land so you could bathe in the river. That was exactly what I'd wanted. But when I reached my claws to the mud, I realized to my mind-numbing horror that I'd forgotten how to write. I was devastated, and panicked. Do you remember how I scraped around, frantically, hoping physical rote memory would take over for my poor, feebled, curse-riddled mind? I think I even rolled in the mud, frustration shutting out all other thought.

Oh, Rivka, Rivka! To have you so close and not be able to tell you!

Then I had another idea, and used my left hand to point to my right hand, hoping you'd recognize the position of my scar. You were kind to me, but I think you said something like, "What's the matter, girl? Did your paw get hurt in the battle?"

Once my mare form had put the idea into your head, it never occurred to you that I was anything but female. Dragons' anatomy is confusing for a beginner, I admit!

I was filled with despair, but then, the very next thing you did was peel off all your clothing to bathe, and I was so overcome that I lost control and turned back into a horse.

Do you remember saying kaddish *for me that night? As a dragon, I curled around you and held you, breaking that you were in such pain, but reveling in the straightforwardness and strength of your love.*

Writing this has calmed me down enough to sleep. I'm leaving this for you to find when you wake up — please let me sleep a little longer so I have enough stamina to carry you and the girls all day.

I love you, and I can't wait to spend the rest of my life with you — NOT AS A HORSE.

Your husband,

Isaac

Chapter 18: The Queen of Perach

The troupe joined the holy women inside the temple for breakfast, and after everyone had eaten, they said their farewells to the sisterhood. Then they were off once more on the dragon's back.

"Thank you for carrying us around this whole time," said the queen, who was riding in front because she was the smallest. "I'm a little bit embarrassed that we work you so hard, now that I know who you are!"

"She rode me into battle for two years," the dragon responded in a booming voice. "I'm used to hard work."

"Your voice sounds different when you're a dragon!" Shulamit tried to quantify the difference — the low tones were louder, somehow, and some of the beauty had fallen away, leaving behind a sort of raw, naked power.

"His voice comes from inside a great cavern now," Aviva observed.

"*Ay yay yay*, I've just figured out that you were in your dragon form when I first came to your door that night in my uncle's castle!" Rivka's head was thrown back in laughter.

"That only took you a whole day," quipped Isaac.

"I'm amazed that you could fit inside in this form!" Rivka exclaimed. "You must have been cramped."

"I was, but I think maybe I found it comforting at the time."

"But then why weren't you squeaky when you were serenading me as a lizard?"

"I used extra magic to be able to use my human voice. Would you have been as impressed with me if I'd spent that whole night with you talking like a lizard?"

"You'd impress me even if you never spoke again," said Rivka, "but I do love listening to your voice."

"You have a wonderful voice," piped up the queen. "I'm not going to make you sing to us when you're already doing so much work to get us home, but I'm looking forward to hearing what that sounds like."

It was very late in the afternoon by the time the travelers reached Ir Ilan, but luckily for Shulamit, most of the stalls in the marketplace were still open. The northerners went off to buy Isaac some new clothes so he wouldn't be stuck wearing a black cassock under the tropical sun, leaving the two younger women on their own. "I got lamb over there last time." Shulamit pointed to the left. "It was pretty good, and I didn't get sick."

"Sounds good to me," said Aviva. "If Riv will let me use one of his smaller knives, I can make a salad for you from those vegetables over there." In public, they were already using all male words for Rivka.

"I'm sure he will — and I'd really like that."

"I'll come with you to get the lamb, first, and then we can pick out our crunchy friends." Aviva followed Shulamit over to the kabob stall, which both scrutinized for any trace of fowl before happily forking over coins with King Noach's picture on them.

"You'll be on the money soon, won't you," Aviva whispered as they left.

"I will! Isn't it weird?"

"Ooh, look at these lovely cucumbers." They were about five inches long and dappled dark green. Aviva began collecting them, while Shulamit swept her gaze over the rest of the vegetables on the table.

"What about onions?" asked the queen.

"Those onions are sweet," the farmer announced proudly.

"Oh, then definitely," said Aviva. "And lemons? Were they able to come to the party today?"

"I don't know what you mean, but I don't have any lemons. You can buy them two stalls down, from the man with the mustache. He's also got lemonade, and mint lemonade too."

They paid the man for the cucumbers and onions and hurried off to the lemon grower. "I'm so glad to be back to this market with you," said Shulamit. "When I was here last week, you kept popping into my head. I thought about how you always liked to shop for your own ingredients to get ideas, and I wished I was here with you."

"That's some wishing power," said Aviva, nuzzling her cheek against Shulamit's since she had too many thing to carry to take her hand.

Shulamit, feeling bold, turned her head and kissed Aviva on the cheek.

"Would you mind not doing that right in front of my shop?" called an unfriendly voice.

Both women started, and looked for the source of the complaint. It was the man with the mustache, the one whose lemons they'd been about to buy. Shulamit felt her face grow hot, and her heartbeat quickened.

"Excuse me?" Aviva asked politely.

"You two. You're disgusting. If everyone was like you, the human race would go extinct."

A poisonous sea began to boil in Shulamit's stomach, and she felt tears of anger spring forth from her eyes. But then she heard familiar voices behind her, one very deep, and both murmuring in the northern tongue — and she knew she was not alone. Still afraid but ignoring it, she took a deep breath, lifted her head, and said haughtily, "Nobody's like me, and you can bet nobody's *ever* been like her — we're pretty amazing!"

"And we don't need lemons that badly if they're going to be as sour as you," Aviva added over her shoulder as they turned around.

Of course, Isaac and Rivka had been right there. Rivka's mask was secure, but it was still easy to tell that she was grinning heartily. "That's the spirit, *Malkeleh!*"

"I'm proud of you," said Isaac, smiling warmly. He had changed into a simple white tunic and trousers, newly purchased at one of the stalls.

"That wasn't fun," said Shulamit, trembling. "But I felt like I could do it because I knew you were there."

"That's what we're here for," said Rivka.

"May God always allow us to be there for you," added Isaac.

Aviva was peering around the marketplace quizzically. "Is anyone else selling lemons?"

❀ • ❀ • ❀

They spent the night at a different inn with a reputation for reliability, and then one more day of traveling put the four of them within the palace walls. It was dark when Isaac finally landed in the garden before the great entrance, but people were

163

still bustling about in the space between dinnertime and sleep. One of the guards, a tall, fit older man with shoulder-length hair, rushed up to greet them.

"Tivon!" Shulamit called out, hopping off Isaac's back and rushing toward him.

"Your Majesty! It's good to see you safe and home. I have news—" Then he broke off, noticing Aviva. "Aviva? Aviva the cook? Wherever did you find her?"

Shulamit waved away the question. "Never mind that for now. Where's Nathan? I have to see him, immediately."

"That's what I was trying to tell you," said Tivon. "He's gone off."

"What?"

"Left early one morning with only a bag of clothing and a sword," said Tivon to the astonished young queen. "His wife woke up and found herself alone. We were all eating breakfast in the courtyard when she came storming in, a babe at her breast, frantic to find him. It was all I could do to comfort her, poor thing."

Shulamit clapped her hands to her face. "The treasury! We have to get to the treasury." She rushed past Tivon into the palace.

Tivon hurried to catch up with her, with Rivka, Aviva, and Isaac in his human form following after. "Your Majesty! What is it?"

"She thinks Nathan stole from her before he left," Rivka called out.

Tivon whipped his head backward. "Stole? Not possible. Others were guarding it that night. Why would you think that?"

"He had already stolen from it once before," said Aviva, "to pay for my mother's surgery. That's how he bribed me to leave the palace."

"I remember him talking about some fool scheme like that," mused the guard. "He knew His Majesty King Noach, may he rest, disapproved of your — er, begging your pardon, Majesty — and thought he would get rewarded for sending you away. He was rewarded with words, not coin, poor wretch. I did wonder where he'd gotten the money from. He was already up to his ears in debt. That's why he left town — to escape the debtors."

"They'll come to scratch at his wife and children, won't they?" asked Aviva.

"I suppose we have to do something for them," said Shulamit, who had stopped rushing around at Tivon's reassurance that the treasury had not been under Nathan's responsibility during the time of his departure. "Oh! My mind is racing from traveling all day and then coming home to such excitement. I've forgotten my manners. Tivon, you've met Riv already, he whom you hired to retrieve me from the kidnappers."

"Yes. I enjoyed his company last week before you left for the temple. Good to see you, sir."

Rivka nodded. "Likewise."

"This is Isaac, his..." Shulamit dithered helplessly.

Sensing Shulamit's panic, Aviva faked a very loud sneeze.

"Isaac's a wizard," Shulamit added. "He'll be added on to the guard as auxiliary."

"Your Majesty, about the guard—" Tivon stopped, his eyes a bit uneasy.

"Yes? You were second-in-command under Nathan," Shulamit pointed out, girding her emotional loins for a conflict. "I suppose you're asking about the captaincy."

"Actually, I am. Your Majesty, I'm set in my ways and don't wish to change my role. I wish to continue serving you and doing my duty, but I don't want the responsibility of heading up the company. I don't want to let you down, but I need to be realistic."

Shulamit relaxed. "This works perfectly — Riv's going to be your new captain."

"Splendid!" Tivon clapped his hands together. "I'll find rooms for you both in the guards' quarters."

"We only need one room," Isaac piped up.

Shulamit and Aviva exchanged pleased looks. For an ordinary man to commit willingly to spending the rest of his life being mistaken for one of them was to win their admiration.

Tivon shrugged. "Fine by me."

Shulamit seized the opportunity to ask, "Tivon, are there any others in the guard who will be unhappy to see Aviva return, now that Nathan's damage has been... patched up?"

Tivon shook his head. "May I speak freely, Your Majesty?" When Shulamit nodded, he continued, "We'd rather your companion be someone we trust, and a resident of the palace. You're our queen and we've sworn to protect you with our lives; however, you have to meet us halfway. Anyone can pose as a willing woman. You simply can't put yourself in a position of that much vulnerability with a stranger. You owe it to your people not to make it that much harder for us to do our jobs."

Shulamit smiled. "I understand now. But I — well, never mind. Aviva's back."

"Will she be rejoining the crew in the kitchen?"

"I'd like to," said Aviva.

"Speaking of kitchens," said Isaac, "I'd like a meal, if that's possible. I should remind you all that I wasn't riding back there with the rest of you." He bestowed upon them a graceful, subtle smirk.

"Hurray! I can be useful again!" cried Aviva with joy. She grabbed his hand and pulled him toward the cooking houses.

Shulamit and Rivka watched them go, Rivka laughing softly to herself.

"Riv?" Tivon's voice broke into their reverie. "Let me show you where to put your things. Then you can go and join your companion in the kitchen."

As Rivka and Shulamit walked back from the guard quarters to the kitchens, they realized they were alone again for the first time in days. "Riv—" said Shulamit, turning toward her on the moonlit path, "thank you. Thank you for everything. I'm so blessed and lucky to have found you — and not just because you brought Aviva back to me. Before our adventure, I felt like an overgrown princess. Now, I know that I can be a proper queen."

"I have to thank you as well," said Rivka gravely. "It makes me sick to think that if I hadn't taken you up on your offer, I'd have grieved for Isaac forever — with him right there under my nose."

"And under your rear," Shulamit quipped.

"See what good comes of helping people?" Rivka pointed out. "Think if you hadn't agreed to help turn the holy women back from stone. And if Aviva hadn't put her mother before herself, you'd never know who stole from your father."

"I'm so glad I gave you that second mango," said Shulamit, grinning. "You remember, back in the Cross-Eyed Tiger? When I bought it I couldn't make up my mind if it was an extra for me, or if it was for you."

"So, *nu*, Queenling — I know this is none of my business, but it will be eventually — have you thought about what you're going to do about producing an heir?"

"A bit," said Shulamit. "Someone in my position can't afford to ignore the question forever. I know it seems like this is my solution for everything, but I was pondering the existence of a young man with my own preferences. He could be Prince Consort, with his own companion, and then I can fulfill my duty to my country."

"How do you propose seeking such a man?"

A sheepish grin spread over Shulamit's face. "I hear there's a mercenary called Riv who's particularly experienced at such things?"

"Oh, you! Well, you'd still have to lie with your prince without pleasure, so you might want to reconsider that plan."

"I did have one other idea," said Shulamit. "You and Isaac might have a baby someday—"

"Never mind, never mind! I think I've heard enough ideas for one night."

Laughing, Rivka followed Shulamit back to the lights of the kitchen house, where both their sweethearts were waiting for them.

END

❀ • ❀ • ❀

Infinite thanks for the following golden souls:

My spouse, for putting up with having these characters move into our apartment with us, and invaluable revising help and advice. Not easy on me, but easy on my spirit.

My mother for introducing me to things like Judaism, Wagner, and feminism, all of which went into the crockpot, and for always making sure I had enough to eat growing up.

My family, for encouragement, Yiddish consulting, and the connection with my heritage.

My amazing cheerleading in-laws, especially Kat.

Katharine "Kate the Great" Thomas O'Gara, for being the kindest, most patient critique partner I could ever ask for, and Dr. Tof Eklund, for always being there to answer random questions even when their schedule was eating them like a rabid three-headed rhino.

Jane, Erika, Rachel, and Mina for their artistic enthusiasm.

Sarah, Rania, Erin, Lorena, Rosie, Beverly, Louise, Dr. Tony Offerle, and Dr. Alana M. Vincent for varied and assorted help.

Bonnie, for believing in my ability to write a novel since before puberty.

Two German musicians, Richard Wagner and René Pape, who inspired me to fly beyond my boundaries.

And finally, Jessica, my stalwart editor; Allison and Jo who helped proofread; and Prizm Books for giving the Perachis a home for three years.

Glossary of non-English words in *The Second Mango*

Some of them seem like English to me, because they were a constant part of my upbringing and remain a constant in my life! But, I realize that many Gentile (non-Jewish) readers would like more information about some of those words, and likewise that not all Jewish readers share my background. It was my hope that I had incorporated them organically, so that they could be understood in context the way one would understand invented words in any other fantasy novel. But why not give people the opportunity to learn more?

The conceit of the Mangoverse is that Perach, the setting, is a Hebrew-speaking haven of tropical agriculture, and that up north, several countries away, there's a country whose primary language is Yiddish. "Perach" itself means "flower" in Hebrew, and is a reference to Perach's being based on South Florida, where I grew up. (Florida also means "flower", in a way.)

What follows is an informal glossary, starting with Chapter 1 of *The Second Mango* and continuing to the end of the book. I don't claim to be an expert in Judaica, but I'd like to offer what I have.

Aba – Dad in Hebrew (Mom is **Ima**)

Malka – Queen (with Malkeleh meaning "little queen", commonly used for a little girl in one's life, even if she's not royalty–the way my dad used to call my little half-sister "Princess." Rivka's use of **Malkeleh** as a pet name for the queen is therefore a pun.)

By the way, the -eleh ending for a name to make a diminutive is a Yiddishism. Shira turns into Shiraleh, for example. And the cat was "ketzeleh" to my grandmother.

So "Malka Shulamit bat Noach" is "Queen Shulamit, daughter of Noach", Noach being her deceased father. "**Bat**"—sounds like *bot* as in robot, not the Halloween flying puppy–is the "daughter of" name syllable. For "son of" it's "**ben**."

The celibate sisters are made up, by the way. They're an imagined offshoot of Judaism that doesn't exist, wearing robes based on Buddhist nuns.Our clergy, as Rivka says in chapter 2 about her own homeland, are **rabbis**. Literally, it means "teacher."

Ir Ilan means Oak Town in Hebrew.

Yom Kippur is the holiest day of the year, the Day of Atonement. It's right after our new year's and it's where you get to get yourself scrubbed clean, spiritually, and promise to do better.There is fasting involved.

Shtik drek = "piece of shit" in Hebrew. "You can't put that in a book!" my grandmother protested. "But she's a *warrior*," I tried to explain…

Nudnik – a Yiddish insult that's hard to define. A lot of these are gonna be like that. The first syllable rhymes with wood.

Putzveytig –Yiddish for "pain in the dick". (You've heard of "putz", right? And veytig = vey is woe or pain or something like that.)

Which reminds me… "**Oy vey**" = literally, Oh woe, so **Oy vey iz mir** is "oh, woe is me." Sounds overdramatic, right? When you've grown up hearing it in another language it just blends in, though.

Mensch = a very decent man. Like, male feminists who actually mean it and aren't just trying to speak over women or get a date. Or my brother-in-law, who feeds the cat when we're on vacations. He is a really good guy.

Shabbat (or **Shabbos**, in Yiddish — Shabbat is Hebrew) is Friday night and Saturday morning. The Jewish Sabbath, involving compulsory rest, special food, candle-lighting, going to **shul** (Yiddish word for temple/synagogue which is the same as the German word for school), and supposedly, marital sex

Seder – the ritual meal associated with **Pesach** (Passover), a really awesome holiday about freedom and human rights and cleaning crumbs off of everything. **Matzo** are big square crackers that have no flavor unless you put things like chopped apples or horseradish dip on them, but fortunately, that's built into the ritual. Yay!

Afikomen – after the seder (see above), the parents hide a matzo wrapped in a napkin (to cut down on the crumbs) somewhere in the house. Then you find it and get a prize. My dad once hid one for me in an orchestral score and then hummed it as my clue. (If you're curious, it was *Till Eulenspiegel*.)

Kippah (Hebrew)/**yarmulke** (Yiddish) – those teensy hats that Jewish men wear in shul and at holidays and weddings.

Mammeh – Yiddish for "Mom". (Dad is "**Tateh**", and they're both the same words in Polish, which makes sense — Yiddish is in a lot of ways Polish-flavored German written in Hebrew letters.)

Kasha varnishkes – buckwheat and butterfly pasta. I don't know what else to say about this besides OM NOM BUCKWHEAT.

Halvah – a sweet desserty thing that is so unbelievably sweet that thinking about it makes me sick. It's shaped like a brick and you break off little pieces and then die of sugar.

Challah – special bread that you make for Shabbat dinner. It's got egg in it, so it's golden, and it's braided, so it's really beautiful.

Howdah – this is NOT Hebrew or Yiddish; this is one of those things you use to ride an elephant with. Since Shulamit's father died by falling off an elephant I needed to use the word. I just didn't want anyone thinking it was Hebrew or Yiddish! Although…. I doubt they have their own words for it, so they'd also probably just say howdah like we do in English.

Nu – it's Yiddish, and it's kind of like "So?" It's a prompting word. Like if you're waiting for someone to answer you and they're just staring into space.

Borscht – Eastern European beet soup. It's BRIGHT POIPLE.

Schmendrick – another one of those undefinable Yiddish insults

Maror – horseradish. Well, "bitter herbs", anyway.

Schreckliches chazzer – dirty pig, in that order. Yiddish.

Fartumult – I asked my grandmother for a word for confused and shocked. This isn't one I heard growing up or anything.

Paskudnyak – Yiddish, an insult, and I'm told it's from Russian.

Ketubah –contract you sign when you get married

Feh – exactly what it sounds like. Snorting dismissively. (Yiddish.)

Kaddish – prayers for the dead. I said them for my dad. (2016 edit: and my grandparents, sigh.)

Ay yay yay – just an exclamation

I hope this helps!

Shira Glassman is a bi Jewish violinist living in Florida with a trans guy labor activist and a badly behaved calico cat. A lifetime of visiting Disney parks while knowing she'd never get to be one of the princesses, plus a steadfast wish to see "knight rescues princess from dragon" reversed to "princess rescues dragon from knight", helped create this book. (Of course, she never expected it to come out as "knight and dragon help the princess save herself!") When not writing fairytales based on her heritage, upbringing, present life, and favorite operas, she can be found on stage or with knitting in hand.

Shira Glassman online:
Blog: http://shiraglassman.wordpress.com
Facebook: http://www.facebook.com/ShiraGlassman
Goodreads:
https://www.goodreads.com/author/show/7234426.Shira_Glassman
Twitter: http://www.twitter.com/shiraglassman

If you liked Shira Glassman's *Tales from Perach*, leaving a review is probably a mitzvah.

Check out the rest of the Mangoverse!

The Second Mango
Climbing the Date Palm
A Harvest of Ripe Figs
The Olive Conspiracy
Tales from Perach/Tales from Outer Lands

Looking for excellent f/f fiction?
Check out:

Daughter of Mystery by Heather Rose Jones
Poppy Jenkins by Clare Ashton

If you're not ready to leave the tropics, try Zen Cho's *Spirits Abroad*

For more Jewish fantasy, try Helene Wecker's *The Golem and the Jinni*

Printed in Great Britain
by Amazon